THE DARKEST KNIGHT

THE CURSED KINGDOM

HILDIE McQUEEN

USA TODAY BESTSELLING AUTHOR

OLIVERHEBERBOOKS

CHAPTER ONE

DUNIMARLE CASTLE
CULROSS, SCOTLAND

It wasn't every day that one traveled to a beautiful medieval country estate in Scotland to rescue a knight in distress. And it certainly wasn't a normal part of Tammie Lockhart's life to be the heroine in a real-life fairytale.

However, needs must and all that stuff.

It didn't seem real, even as she walked to the front door of the castle that her sisters, Gwen and Sabrina, called home since Gwen had married a real-life handsome laird. That this particular hunky laird was from the sixteen hundreds, and Gwen had rescued him, was a story she didn't have time to delve into at the moment.

The entryway was straight out of a movie set with a high ceiling and tapestries depicting hunting scenes or people frolicking about in the outdoors hanging on the thick stone walls.

Her feet sank into the thick plush rug, and she glanced down to note the design of huge bouquets of roses seeming to be tossed haphazardly and yet creating a beautiful scene.

On her right was an archway that led to what she would call a large sitting room furnished with couches, chairs, and tables that were grouped in different areas for easy conversation.

To the left, just past the sitting room, was another archway into a dining room with a long mahogany table that could easily sit twelve.

Continuing forward, the next doorway opened to the library, where she and her sisters spent many an hour working on what had become the most important project of their lives.

Sabrina, who was engaged to a man named Gavin Campbell, would probably be in the library, Tammie considered.

She pictured Gavin again, a walking golden god that had to be the most beautiful human being in existence. Her soon-to-be brother-in-law's good looks were no exaggeration, as wherever he was seen, people would stop mid-sentence, mid-bite, even mid-step and gawk, their conversation, food, and destination instantly forgotten.

Thankfully, the guy was an introvert, who preferred spending time at the stables in the company of the horses and an older man named Miles.

"There you are." Sabrina poked her head out of the library doorway and grinned at her. "I think I found something. Come and read this."

Despite the direness of the situation, Tammie considered making a run for the kitchen. The cook, chef, or whatever the man liked to be called, had baked a delicious cake the night before and she was anxious to gobble another piece.

"Can it wait until I cut myself a slice of cake?" Tammie called out.

"No," came the abrupt answer.

Upon entering the library, she found that Gwen was there as well. The eldest sister sat on an overstuffed chair, her ebony hair twisted into a messy bun that didn't distract from her Instagram-ready beauty. Not that Gwen had ever been on social media.

Gwen's dark gaze lifted to Tammie as she walked through the door. "Something must be done to convince Niall to assist in his own rescue. It seems he wishes to remain behind, stuck there in that horrible place."

Nail MacTavish had been plunged into an enchantment by an evil wizard after he and four others, including Tristan and Gavin, thwarted his plans to snatch defenseless women from a village. The men had been stuck in another realm, a place filled with peril and danger for hundreds of years.

The entire situation was beyond belief. Even after her sisters had freed two men, Tammie still had a hard time accepting that the reality of alter-worlds, other realms.

And yet, not only was it real, but now it was her turn to save someone.

Just before being trapped, a powerful enchantress had managed to cast a spell that made it possible to break each man's curse. Figuring out how to break each of their spells was not easy, even harder in Niall's case because he refused to cooperate, claiming he preferred to remain in the other realm until death.

As much as Tammie wanted to free him, at the same time, it was a bit frightening to find out what Niall's particular curse was. Not only that, but she had to come up with a spell to break the curse, and somehow do this within a short time, as the possibility of the men being trapped forever came near.

Despite the looming deadline and the dilemma of what to do about the trapped men, at the moment her life could not be more perfect. She was assistant to her sister Sabrina, who was a well-known and extremely well-paid fashion photographer. Just recently she'd hooked up with Gerard, a handsome model, and if she read things right, they were on the brink of formalizing their relationship.

Not only that, but her handmade and personally designed online jewelry business was thriving. Yes, her life was definitely on the right track.

Lastly, there was the bonus of spending time with her sisters in an honest to goodness castle in a small town in the most beautiful country she'd ever visited.

Everything couldn't be more perfect.

Well, except for the reluctant knight in distress.

"NIALL HAS good reason to be the way he is. I can't imagine the grief he suffered at not only losing his wife, but his children as well. All because of an act of nobility," Gwen said interrupting Tammie's thoughts.

"Saving that village from a wizard's curse on that day sealed their fate," Sabrina added.

Tammie shuddered. "Not only that but being trapped in another realm for hundreds of years is horrible."

"I understand Niall grieves, but he needs to give himself permission to live. It's been hundreds of years," Sabrina quipped, plopping down on the floor and stretching like a cat.

Despite loving life at the castle, Tammie had no plans to remain longer than necessary. "We have to consider if there is another reason why he is reluctant to be rescued. Maybe the idea of coming back here to a totally different time, where everything has changed, terrifies him."

Gwen shook her head. "I told Tristan that if Niall doesn't wish to be rescued, then it may be impossible to do so. My poor dear refuses to accept the idea of leaving a man behind."

"Maybe we can move on to the other guy, Padriag. He wants to be rescued," Tammie suggested.

"Unfortunately he hasn't felt a pull to come here. It isn't his time yet," Gwen replied. "It is Niall's turn. It has to be done in order."

Tammie crossed her arms, tapping her fingers on her upper arms with impatience. "Then he's coming out. I will do it with or without his help."

Her sisters exchanged a look.

She narrowed her eyes at them. "What?"

"This is going to be an interesting one," Gwen said looking past her, not meeting her gaze.

Sure she missed something, she gave them one last

piercing look before she closed her eyes, tried to picture the knight in question, and began calling for him.

She'd been told Niall MacTavish was tall, dark and a classically handsome man, According to Sabrina, who was particularly good at describing people, given her work, Niall stood at about six two, with broad shoulders, the blackest hair she'd ever seen and piercing grey eyes the color of a stormy sky. Her sister had pronounced him to be "stunning", which was saying a lot.

Trying her best to picture him, she recalled having been told that he seemed to sport a scowl constantly. Chanting, she called to him, feeling the connection almost immediately.

The room seemed to shift; she opened her eyes and saw that someone had appeared.

Liam, a lean blonde man stood before them. Dressed in clothing more suited for medieval times, he looked around the room and nodded in greeting to her sisters. His blue eyes landed on her and studied her briefly before speaking.

"Niall refuses to come."

Tammie shook her head. "Liam, I told you to threaten him with bringing me back to the realm if he didn't come here. Did you?"

Her sisters looked at her with rounded eyes. Gwen spoke up first. "Tammie, you can't go there, it's much too dangerous."

"If you continue to summon him, he will have to come eventually," Liam said. "He is beginning to fade in and out as it is." He laughed. "Of course that means he is in a rather cross mood, not liking how you affect him."

"Angrier than usual? How can you tell?" Sabrina asked.

"In that you are correct, Niall seems to be in a continuous bad mood as of late."

Sabrina's anxious eyes met hers. "Tammie give him a couple days. Then, if he doesn't come, you will probably be forced to go to the alter-world."

Tammie raised her gaze to Liam. "How long before you go to Atlandia?" she asked, referring to a region in the alter-world ruled by two queens who were somewhat friendly.

"Could be a few days yet," Liam replied.

"Then I think I should go today. I'll stay until you are forced to move to Atlandia. I don't want to go to that place. It should be named Icelandia from what I've heard." Tammie headed for the door. "Somebody help me pack. Is there a weight limit to moving between realms Liam?"

Liam did not reply, and she turned to look at him. The British knight seemed to be looking to her sisters for an answer.

Gwen shook her head. "Once a Lockhart makes up her mind, there is nothing to be done. If she says she is going with you, then Tammie will."

Chapter Two

The darkness enveloped Niall and he fought against it with all his might. Clawlike fingers reached for him, raking into his skin, tearing his flesh away from muscle and bone, leaving a stinging trail of pain down his legs, back and arms.

Laughter echoed, bouncing off the dirty, vermin-infested cell. The sound rang in his ears until he thought he'd scream.

The time had come. He had gone mad. He'd finally lost his mind, and he almost welcomed it.

Would the unfairness of his life go with him into the madness that enveloped him? Would the memories remain unscathed?

At the moment, he not only remembered everything he wanted to forget, but each single memory was magnified. Each painful experience of his past so real it was worse than any physical pain.

The assault abruptly ended, and he collapsed on the dirt floor, his breathing labored. Without warning, an invisible, vise-like hold tightened around his body pinning him against the damp, muddy wall.

What was left of his ragged, bloody clothing was torn from his body before the hold loosened, and once again Niall crumpled onto the floor.

Naked as a newborn babe, he inched back into a corner, straining both eyes and ears.

Finally, light from a torch flickered in the distance and moved closer. A woman appeared. She was dressed in light, flowing clothing which contrasted sharply against the muck and dirt of the dungeons. She seemed to glide toward his cell, passing the iron bars as if they didn't exist.

The smell that reminded him of burning cedar and fragrant lilies assaulted his nose.

"Look at me Niall." Her voice vibrated with anger. Her black eyes pierced his when he lifted his gaze. "It doesn't have to be like this every time. You can just give yourself to me willingly." Her lips curved into a smile that was somehow more malevolent than when she sneered. "Our encounters would be so much more enjoyable for you."

Niall struggled to his feet backing against the corner of the dirty, stinking cell. Despite the fact the woman always won, he would never stop fighting.

Despite the suffering his actions brought, her obvious sting at being rejected was enough of a reward.

Whatever she was, witch or demon, Devina, as she called herself, was as beautiful as she was evil.

Not long after arriving in the alter-world, during one of Meliot's quests, he'd come across Devina. The demon had pretended to need rescue, and to his ill-luck, he'd been the one to take her upon his steed and ride to where she lived. Since that fated day, she'd bewitched him with a powerful spell, binding him to her.

"Full of chatter as usual, Lover?" She closed the distance and ran a long fingernail down the center of his chest.

"I am speaking to you!" Devina screamed and when he remained silent, slapped him hard across the face. "Do you have any idea how many males desire me? And yet, you act as if being near me is a burden."

With a huff, she motioned two large males he'd not seen arrive to come forward. "Ensure that he learns not to ignore me when I speak to him." Her eyes slid slowly over his body, hesitating on his limp cock. She arched a brow. "I'll see you in my chamber." She moved away, taking the torch and his ability to see with her.

Grunts told him her henchmen moved closer, and he held his fists up, prepared to fight. When the first lash of the whip struck, the sting shocked him. The second and third hit in rapid succession. He was at a disadvantage. They could see in the dark.

The lashings continued until darkness claimed him.

NIALL WOKE to find he was on Devina's bed, satin sheets covered his nakedness. The sound of liquid being poured made his mouth water, and he turned his head to see that she was standing next to the bed, pouring a glass of wine.

Without offering him a drink, she took a long swallow, her eyes raking over his chest. He glanced down knowing not a mark from his torture would be evident. Devina didn't like any visible marks on him. Her magic always left him perfectly healed without even a scar after his time in the dungeons.

"Will you make love to me today?" Always the same question, and he never answered. Instead, he looked away, studying the ever-changing décor of the room. Today the walls were blood red, the bed coverings black as night. A statue of Venus, with her eyes blindfolded, was evidence of Devina's mood.

When he was about to ask for water, she pinned him with her gaze and slowly removed the sash that held her robe in place and allowed the silky fabric to fall from her shoulders. He turned away, refusing to acknowledge the evil woman. She laughed, a shrill, mirthless sound. "What is the matter, Lover? You don't appreciate what most men would give an eye tooth for?"

An invisible forced pulled his arms up over his head. Sashes manifested, wrapping around his wrists and the headboard. Another set appeared at his ankles, his legs spread as the fabric was tied to opposing bedposts.

He struggled against the restraints, but only half-heartedly, hoping to save his energy to fight against her.

Devina climbed on the bed, and straddled him, sitting on his thighs. "How about we play pretend?" She held up a black sash, her dark eyes twinkling mischievously. She blindfolded him and waited a few beats. "I am her, the one you desire."

A vision of a petite blonde woman slammed into his mind, and he was so astounded he let out a gasp. What trick was this?

When he didn't harden, the demon screeched with rage.

"All you have to do is give yourself to me, then you will be free. Just do it!" her furious screech made his ears ring.

He wouldn't cede. The demon lied. Nail knew down to his bones that if he gave himself to her, the tie would become stronger.

Thump, thump, thump ... the constant sound vibrated through the keep. He was back in his bedchamber. Back in the keep he'd shared with the other four knights for centuries. Niall rolled over his breaths like pants as relief washed over him.

The thumping continued as he slid out of the bed and pulled his breeches on. He stormed out of the room and down the stairs. "Padriag!"

Thump, thump, thump, the sounds continued.

He went down the stairs stopping on the landing just as the basketball flew past his shoulder. It bounced off the wall back toward the red-face young knight who grabbed it and eyed him with distaste.

"You could have caught that." Padriag said, beginning to bounce it again, turning away from him.

Niall rushed to him and grabbed him by the scruff, picking the sweaty man off the ground. "I was trying to sleep." He shoved the younger man away watching him stumble, barely able to keep from falling.

Padriag whirled around rubbing the back of his neck. "I don't know why you're such an ass. You went to your room early last night. How many damn hours of sleep do you need?"

Without responding, Niall went to the large dining table and sat. Noticing a pot of tea, he poured himself a cup. "Where is Liam?"

If everyone was to be rescued one by one from this realm, Niall was perturbed at the idea of being left to live alone with Padriag. The young knight who'd been only two and twenty when enchanted remained a reckless youth.

With his joy in life barely dimming over the years and his ability to find humor in almost every situation, Padriag was his complete opposite. Niall didn't begrudge the young man's refusal to see the worst, for Padriag had suffered alongside him at Meliot's hands, just as much as the others.

But most times, Padriag's constant cheery disposition grated at him, reminding him of his constant torment even more.

"Liam went to the other realm to see your enchantress. She's been summoning you," Padraig told him. "If I were you I would go. She's threatened on more than one occasion to come here."

"It's too dangerous," Niall replied, "I do not believe Tristan or Gavin will allow her to come here."

Tamara, the woman who was to supposedly free him from his enchantment, was wasting her time. He would never leave. There would never be freedom for him, whether there in the alter-world or in the other realm.

Padriag went to a narrow window and peered out. "The watchdogs looked bored. Some of them are asleep. No orders to storm the keep today, I suppose. Either that or they can't get past my mighty wards." He held up his arms flexing his biceps, and then began a warding spell, dashing about the room, using his magical powers to fortify the wards of protection he'd installed and maintained since they arrived in the alter-world.

Niall watched him for a moment. Soon Meliot's minions would storm the keep. Meliot was a powerful wizard and could probably dispose of Padriag's wards easily. Once the keep was overtaken, they'd be forced to leave. To move to Atlandia where the royal overseers would grant them asylum in exchange for joining their forces of shifters and sentries against Meliot's dark forces.

Chapter Three

Tammie pulled out a small backpack she'd grabbed from Gwen's room earlier and began looking around the room deciding what to take. Was the alter-world cold or warm? Did she need to bring sweats or shorts?

Where was Gwen? Her older sister had traveled to the alter-world when rescuing her handsome husband, Tristan.

No sign of anyone approaching, so she settled for a pair of worn jeans and a t-shirt and stuffed them into the pack. She went to the small bathroom and grabbed toothpaste and a toothbrush. After a few minutes she decided to grab a deodorant and a small bottle of body lotion.

Tammie walked back into the bedroom and screamed, dropping her toiletries in her fright.

Niall stood by the bed, glaring down at the backpack.

"You actually meant to come to the other realm?" he asked in deep, heavily accented Scottish tones.

"Y-you startled me," Tammie stammered, crouching down and picking the dropped items off the floor.

He opened the backpack and peered inside. "How long were you planning to stay? You are not packing very much."

His clothing that consisted of a tunic and leather pants, was interesting. Somehow, his way of dress suited his wide-shouldered, well-built frame. Then again, the man would look good in just about anything.

She shoved the toiletries into the backpack. "As long as it takes to convince your stubborn self to tell me what the terms of breaking your enchantment are." Tammie jutted out her chin and looked up at him.

"That is not enough clothing for two hundred years."

"You do realize that the sooner we break your curse, the sooner Padriag can be rescued. Not only that, but then the others can go on with their lives." Tammie let out a slow breath before continuing. "Don't you think it's time for everyone to be happy?"

"Yes. I do." His brows drew together, his lips pressed into a tight line. When they locked gazes, Tammie was the first to look away. "Do you not have a husband you should be with?"

"I am not married," Tammie replied. "But I do not plan to stay here trying to help you for two hundred years. Besides, at the most I have about sixty years tops left to live." She snorted at her joke.

He scowled, but did not say anything.

"Do you have a lover?"

Interesting that he'd ask that. "What difference does that make?" Tammie sat on the edge of the bed and frowned. "I do have a man in my life. His name is Gerard."

"Return to him and leave me. I am where I want to be."

"Really?" Tammie asked and glared up at him. "You want to stay in that place? All alone without your friends? You want to give up on ever having a family, a normal life?"

The storm in his eyes made her wish she'd not spoken. He'd had a life, a family, and lost it all.

"My reasons are my own. I know what is best for me. There are things that even breaking from the enchantment would not change about my life."

Tammie found herself at a loss as to how to help him. "Have you explained to the others why you don't want to leave? Because honestly, I don't get it."

"No. There is nothing to explain."

Stubborn, stubborn man.

Tammie decided to change tactics. "What about Padriag? What if his enchantment terms are tied to you?"

"I doubt it. The conditions of his enchantment have nothing to do with me."

"Has he told you the terms of his enchantment?"

His nodded. "All of us know the rules for breaking his enchantment by heart. The lad never stops talking."

Tammie smiled. "I have not met him. He sounds nice from what the others say about him. Can he leave the enchantment and appear here?"

"Perhaps. He leaves and goes back to his ancestral home quite often." The familiar scowl returned. "I must go."

His abrupt announcement caught her by surprise. "Oh, no. You can't. Not yet." Tammie grabbed onto his sleeve. "I can't let you leave until you promise to return and discuss the situation again. Otherwise, I will come to you."

Niall's eyes locked to where she held onto his arm. She fisted the fabric tighter, hoping he couldn't disappear if she hung on to his clothing. Then, not satisfied, she grabbed his hand with her free one and held her breath. Just in case he decided to flash away, she'd be semi-prepared.

"Why do you close your eyes?"

Tammie opened them. "I was preparing myself in case you left and took me with you."

He didn't respond, but she noticed his gaze flickered from her face to their intertwined fingers. "You can release me. I will return."

"Tomorrow."

"Aye, tomorrow."

"Promise?"

"I promise."

Still not sure, she released his shirt, but not his hand. "I don't know if I trust you." She studied him. "I need some kind of insurance."

He rolled his eyes.

Adorable. It was the first time he'd shown any kind of an almost fun gesture. Tammie caught herself and scowled at him.

"What are you two doing?" Liam stood at the doorway. Gwen and Sabrina's faces peeked around him.

The blonde knight smiled at noticing their clutched hands and earned a growl from Niall who tried to pull his hand free of Tammie's. She hung on to it.

"I won't release him until he swears to return tomorrow," Tammie explained to the group.

"I've promised," Niall retorted through gritted teeth.

Tammie looked to her sisters who both studied Niall. "Should I trust that he will do as he's promised?"

Sabrina pushed past Liam and moved closer. "I don't know, I think he has too. Some kind of knight rule." She turned to Liam. "Am I right?"

"Why don't you ask him?" Liam replied, obviously enjoying Niall's discomfort.

Everyone looked to Niall who in turn looked straight ahead to the blank wall. "I must keep my word. It is part of the Knight's code."

"There you see," Gwen, ever the trusting soul, told Tammie. "Let him go. He looks like he's in pain."

"He's not in pain." Tammie stood on her tiptoes and studied his face. "Are you?"

A muscle on the side of his jaw pulsed, and Tammie bit her bottom lip. "Oh goodness maybe he's got a headache."

At Liam's loud laugh they all turned to him. "He's not sick, he's mad. Furious in fact."

Tammie yelped and released Niall's hand jumping away from him. "Jeez. Once you're free we're taking you to see someone about anger management."

Niall looked at her for a long moment. For those few seconds it was as if no one else in the room existed. She was surprised that anger was not present in his eyes, but instead a deep longing and something else, an emotion that she could only describe as sadness.

"Well ladies, we must bid you farewell for now. Niall will be here tomorrow."

Both knights disappeared.

Niall never looked away from her.

Chapter Four

After hours of Liam and Padriag going on and on about the virtues of the other realm, Niall was more convinced he wouldn't go. To be back in the world he'd once known, where he'd planned to raise a family and grow old with a wife, the stark reality of Devina in his life would only make him more miserable.

Finally, after pretending to relent by stating he'd think about it, the two did stop their quest to change his mind.

Each night he had but one prayer, that Devina would not come to him, and he could have an entire night of sleep.

Thankfully, that night he slept without interruption. Usually after Devina's visits, she didn't come to him for several nights.

A loud boom sounded, and Niall jumped from his bed and rushed to look out. It had finally happened. Meliot's minions had breached the safeguard and would soon be descending upon their keep. Gavin and Tristan's escape had angered the wizard, and he was determined to keep the rest of them captive.

What the wizard wasn't aware of was that Liam's curse had also been broken, and the Englishman was free. Unlike the other free men, Liam was able to traverse between the realms and had agreed to remain in the alter-world to keep his escape a secret.

"They've broken through!" Padriag called out, appearing at Niall's bedroom door. "We must leave at once."

Once dressed, both men rushed to a doorway in the back of the keep. It was very possible the attackers had surrounded the keep, but there was a small inner garden that would allow them to dematerialize and get away before it was reached.

With swords in hand, they raced down the stairs and into the great room. Liam was already downstairs waiting.

"The horses are east, I managed to get them to the woods."

Together they went to the back door, and Niall pushed it open, only to slam it shut at seeing several creatures had climbed over the wall.

"The roof!" he yelled.

It wasn't long before they got to the opening to the roof. Although Meliot had dragons, they'd not heard the tell-tale signs of their ear-piercing screeches.

Once again, being the strongest, Niall pushed the heavy metal hatch open and peered out. "They're not here yet. Hurry."

No sooner did they emerge onto the rooftop, than claws appeared over the ledge.

Without hesitating, they dematerialized and reappeared in the forest.

They came upon their horses only a few yards away. The steeds were not only covered in thick fur-lined blankets across their backs, but their legs were also wrapped in the same. Plush cloaks were thrown across the saddles for the men and they donned the warm coverings and mounted. As if sensing the urgency, the horses broke into a gallop, the huge beasts using every inch of their muscular legs to cross the distance between the keep and their destination.

They had to escape to Atlandia, a treacherous zone that was protected by ice storms that could freeze most humans in less than a pair of hours.

Once they crossed the border into Atlandia, they would be relatively safe. Not only was the threat of the icing a deterrent, but the royals kept huge wolf sentries that attacked intruders without hesitation.

Padriag studied the sky. "We have to make it to Atlandia before the first sun sets and The Icing begins."

Looking up, Niall noticed there were two suns that day, one lower in the sky. By its position in the sky, it would be several hours before it would no longer be visible.

Already the wind was frigid, and he pulled the hood up over his head. The thick cloak helped, but nothing withstood the freezing temperatures that were accompanied by sleet so sharp it felt as if it cut through a person's skin.

"Keep an eye out for the sentries," Liam said, the blond Englishman's head swiveling from side to side. "I sense them near." Liam had been gifted with foresight by the powerful enchantress who had tried to help them when they'd been enchanted.

The enchantress had tried valiantly, but hadn't been able to break their curses, yet somehow managed to give each of them a gift. Padriag had the gift of simple magic like warding and making things disappear. Niall had received the gift of healing others, Tristan the gift of strength, and Gavin the gift of seduction, much to his chagrin.

As they climbed a steep ridge, a shortcut to the castle where they'd seek refuge, the road became perilous. Despite trudging slowly, more than once, the horses slipped, the brave animals managing to remain upright.

Atlandia was a treacherous land, dangerous as it was beautiful. Tall snow-covered mountains flanked the horizon, the forest, although snow covered, was lush and majestic.

Moments later the road became barely visible as the sleet sliced through the air, the shards falling like icy sheets from the darkened sky. The falling ice was accompanied by a howling wind.

The Icing had begun.

Niall leaned over the horse, making himself as flat as possible to keep his face covered. Thankfully, the horses wore head guards that kept their eyes protected, else they too would be unable to see.

"The sun is setting," Padriag screamed as loud sounds like thunder boomed overhead.

"It hasn't set enough, unfortunately," Niall called back. "Soon it will get worse."

Liam waved an arm and held up a hand, signaling for

them to stop. "Sentries should be appearing soon. Can you do something to let them know who we are?" he asked Padriag.

"Three humans traversing into the Icing should be a pretty big hint that we are idiots and therefore not a threat," Padriag replied dryly. "I can make us invisible, but it won't hold for long in these conditions."

"Let us continue forward whilst keeping a steady pace," Niall suggested.

It was hard to keep his teeth from chattering. The air felt as if he was dunked into an ice bath. Despite the cloak and warmth of the horse, he couldn't stop the shivering. The horses seemed impervious to the cold, and he wondered if it had to do with the fact they were from that realm. The animals continued forward, their exhalations steaming in the air.

Glancing over to Liam and Padriag, he noted both men, like him, rode with their bodies flat against their horses. If they didn't arrive to shelter soon, they would not survive much longer.

The winds shifted in direction, the sleet lessened, and finally, Niall could make out mountains to the west, which shielded the castle they were headed to. Thankfully, they'd been heading in the right directions, however, they were still at least an hour's ride away.

Pulling his cloak tighter, he scanned the trees for the royal sentries. Movement caught his attention, and he concentrated on the area to ensure his eyes weren't playing tricks.

"I think I see something moving," Liam said, confirming

that there was something or someone watching from the edge of the forest.

Moments later, a pack of enormous wolves seemed to materialize out of thin air. Their light gray and white fur perfectly blending with the background. The largest of the wolves, whose shoulders were as high as the top of the horse's legs, neared and shook snow and ice from its huge head. The wolf's light blue eyes met Niall's.

They were the royal sentries, all shifters of some sort. This large wolf who stood before the rest of the pack had to be the shifter called Argo.

"Argo, we are here to ask for asylum from your rulers," Padriag called out. "We had to flee from our home. It was attacked by Meliot's forces."

The wolf's head slowly turned to Padriag, its eyes narrowing. Meliot and the royals of Atlandia were mortal enemies, although they'd lived in relative peace for the last decade or so, with each side ensuring they kept within the boundaries of their lands.

The wolf seemed to nod, then turned to face the pack. The wolves then formed two lines, leaving just enough room for the three men on horseback to continue in a single file.

Escorted by the wolves, the horses seemed to feel protected because they moved forward at a faster speed until galloping with the wolves easily keeping pace.

Niall wanted to cry in relief when the huge gray stone castle came into view, the magnificent structure a beacon of warmth and safety. He prayed the princesses within were amenable to allowing them to stay. The rulers were sisters,

Rubiana and Esmeralda, identical except for the colors they wore. Both blonde, Rubiana always wore blood red, whilst her sister was usually draped in deep green.

Flanked by the wolf sentries, they traversed a bridge to arrive at massive gates upon which another group of wolves appeared, their yellow eyes seeming to glow in the darkness.

It was strange how these beings seemed impervious to the freezing temperatures of Atlandia.

Their guardians lifted their heads, seeming to communicate with the gate guardians because the massive structures began opening at once.

Passing into the courtyard was a shock to the senses. Huge bonfires warmed the surroundings, a welcome reprieve from the frigid temperatures outside. Niall looked up almost expecting to see some sort of dome that kept the heat in place. The only thing above was the cloudy sky with only one sun barely visible.

A large male approached, wearing a thick cloak over what Niall guessed was a naked body. He recognized Argo, who's neutral expression was neither menacing, nor welcoming. The male waited for Niall, Liam and Padriag to dismount and then signaled to others, who took their horses away.

"They will be warm in the stables," Argo stated in a deep voice. "Meliot has attacked your keep before. What was different this time that you seek refuge?"

Although Niall understood the male was in charge of the royal's security, the questioning still angered him.

The more diplomatic Liam replied. "We are not from this realm and are limited in protecting ourselves from creatures here. Those who attacked today were much stronger and with powers we cannot defend against. Two of our group have broken away from this realm. We believe it angers Meliot."

If Argo was surprised at the news that two of them had left, he gave no indication. Instead he nodded in understanding. "Follow me."

They entered through an arched entryway and down a short corridor that was lit with sconces along the walls. The floor was padded with thick carpeting. They followed Argo into a space that was not unlike the largest room at their keep. Inside was a long table flanked by ten chairs on each side. Long buffet cabinets on both sides of a huge fireplace graced one wall, and on the opposite stood a dais of sorts with a shorter, intricately carved table in front of three, just as decorative chairs with tall backs.

A thin man dressed simply in a tunic and long leather breeches hurried into the room, followed by two women with a tray in each hand. The man motioned to the long table in the center of the room. "Welcome gentlemen; I hope your travels were not too perilous."

Obviously a servant of sorts, the man seemed anxious to please. He moved around behind them as they, along with Argo, settled into chairs, then the women placed trays with bowls of warm water and cloths for them to wipe their faces and hands.

"A meal will be brought for you straight away," the thin man stated, his eyes following their every move. Once everyone made use of the water and cloths, the thin man signaled for the women to remove the trays as he poured from a pitcher into their goblets.

"Hot spiced wine to warm you," the thin man informed them and then added. "I am Fitz, at your service, for whatever you require."

Padriag drank from the goblet and then looked at Argo. "Does this mean we are granted asylum?"

"Their highnesses had agreed to give you asylum when Tristan asked during a visit. We expected you would come … eventually," the wolf shifter replied and leaned back into the chair, drinking deeply from his goblet. "I am sure they will speak to you tomorrow."

The rich aroma of spices wafted through the air just before the same pair of women returned. One set a basket filled with enticing loaves of bread between them, the other woman placed deep bowls of a thick broth with chunks of meat and what looked to be carrots and potatoes in front of each of them.

Despite not thinking he was hungry, Niall ate every bit of the stew and an entire loaf of the freshly baked bread.

Their goblets were refilled as they ate, and they drank their fill.

"We appreciate the princesses' hospitality," Niall said to Argo, who nodded in response.

"Can I ask," Padriag said, "why do you seem impervious to the cold?"

Argo's large shoulders lifted and lowered. "Our species is native to this region. Some of us do not live in structures, but out in the wild, or in huts. We have thick undercoats to keep us warm. We are bred for surviving here."

"Makes sense. That's awesome," Padriag replied.

"If you are ready, I will show you to your bedchambers," Fritz exclaimed in a tone that was much too cheerful for the occasion.

Leaving Argo in the dining room, they followed the thin man up a stairwell to the third level and there they were shown a large chamber. The first thing Niall noticed was that they would be sharing a set of rooms. The spacious bedroom had four beds and next to it was a small sitting room and another room he assumed was a bathroom.

Padriag made a beeline for the bathroom. "I wonder if they have running water." The knight peered into the room. "Nope, there's a basin and several large pitchers full of water and chamber pots. I hate chamber pots."

Only one thing worried Niall. Would Devina find him there? If so, what would occur if his friends tried to wake him during the time she had taken him away in his sleep? How could he possibly keep the secret of what happened to him?

Liam studied him. "Is something wrong Niall?"

Looking around the room, he tried to figure out which bed would serve him best. "I do not like being here. Having to seek asylum for the rest of our days here."

"I foresee something interesting," Liam began. Niall froze, not wanting to hear what Liam had to say. The Brit's abilities to see the future was yet another thing to worry about.

"I see you going places, some sort of travel," Liam continued. "It's probably just your trips back and forth to see Tamara."

Padriag walked out of the bathroom, a chamber pot in hand. "So what the hell am I supposed to do with this?"

"Put it back," Liam yelled, "For god's sakes, I know you didn't just walk out carrying your shit. They have servants to clean up."

"So I just leave it?" Padriag scowled. "Fine, but it's going to be stinky in there."

"It is getting smelly in here," Liam retorted, holding his nose. "Go away."

***

AFTER AN EVENTLESS NIGHT, Niall woke and stretched from under the thick coverlets in a bed so comfortable, it was tempting not to complain about staying there for the foreseeable future.

Liam was sitting up in his bed, his blond hair askew, a frown between his brows. "I will have to return to the other realm in a few days."

Having met his partner, a man called John Stewart, Liam's dour disposition had softened significantly. That Liam remained more in this realm, to help the two who remained there, was admirable.

"I want coffee," Padriag said with a loud yawn. "I bet they don't have coffee here."

Throughout the many years trapped in the alter-world, Padriag was the one who'd kept in touch with the changes in society. He spoke in modern English, which admittedly was helpful. However, the knowledge of how things had changed meant Padriag was constantly complaining about the lack of amenities in this realm.

After a knock on the door, Fritz and the ever present two women entered the room. "Good morn gentlemen. I have fresh clothing for you to wear when greeting my princesses. Once you have completed your morning ablutions, I will accompany you to the throne room."

The women walked out and returned with bowls of warm water and cloths; then they walked out.

"I will be right outside," Fritz announced with a wide grin, he walked out and closed the door.

"That guy is way too cheerful. Its creepy," Padriag grumbled.

FROM HIS POSITION on bended knee, Niall looked up at the two princesses. Their breathtaking beauty did not distract from their distant royal demeanor. The sisters waited for them to plead their case although they were already aware of why they were there.

"Your Highnesses, Sir Padriag Clarre, Sir Liam Murray and I, Niall McTavish, Duke of Lennox humbly request asylum from you and your people. In exchange for our swords which we pledge to you."

"Please rise," Rubiana, the princess robed in red, told them. The three knights stood, hands on the hilts of their swords signaling fidelity to the crown.

"You come at a good time." The other princess' gaze fell on him. Esmeralda's ice blue gaze shone unnaturally, and he wondered what kind of entity the princesses were, and if they also were able to shift as well. "Our villages on the valley side have been attacked by Meliot's minions. They have defended themselves valiantly, but it's time for us to put a stop to this."

Rubiana addressed them next. "In two days we will dispatch guards to Middlesex for protection and to ensure that when Meliot's fighters appear, they learn our people are not without protection."

She looked over to where Argo stood to the side of the thrones. "These noblemen will travel with you to Middlesex."

"If I may be so bold to ask another favor," Niall asked before they were dismissed.

"Speak, knight," Esmeralda said, curiosity evident as she leaned forward.

"I request permission for us to go to another realm from within the castle walls. We have business to attend to there that is important in our fight against Meliot."

The princesses looked at one another, both silent. Niall suspected by their cocked heads that they communicated telepathically. Finally, Rubiana looked at him. "Permission is granted, but you must wait until after returning from Middlesex."

That was not an acceptable option. Niall went to speak but Liam cleared his throat, and he hesitated.

"Your Highnesses, if I may be so bold as to request that at least one of us be able to return to the other world if only to advise our allies about what happens."

Again the Princesses were silent. Neither seemed too perturbed at Liam's request. One thing about the Brit, his demeanor always seemed to smooth the way for easier negotiations of any kind.

"Permission is granted. Send the young one," Rubiana told them.

Niall ground his teeth. He'd given his word to Tamara. A knight did not break his word.

Wolves approached.

They'd been dismissed.

Chapter Five

Tammie stomped up the stairs, her heels echoing like tiny thunderclaps, frustration bubbling with every step. She was on a mission to find Gwen, though her anger dulled to a simmer as she approached her sister's bedroom door. She paused, her hand on the doorknob. Gwen and Tristan were always ... well, occupied. Bursting in might not be her wisest move.

Instead, she knocked lightly. "Gwen?"

"Come in," her sister called out, her voice calm and inviting.

Tammie poked her head in. The late afternoon light spilled through the window, casting a warm glow over the room. Gwen sat serenely in a chair by the window, her fingers idly tracing the armrest, while Tristan lounged opposite her. His broad shoulders and imposing frame made the chair look comically undersized, as if it might collapse beneath him at any moment. At Tammie's entry, Tristan stood, his movements fluid despite his size, and offered a small bow.

"Hello, Tamara. Is everything well?" His deep, velvety voice filled the room, carrying an old-world charm.

"Tristan!" Gwen scolded, shooting him a look. "Modern English, remember?"

He smirked, his hazel eyes alight with mischief, before turning back to Tammie. His smile—an easy, lopsided grin—could have melted stone. "Hi, Tammie. What's up?"

Gwen giggled, her cheeks glowing as she glanced at him. They were annoyingly adorable together.

Tristan stretched his arms over his head. "I have work to do, so I'll leave you two to talk." He leaned down, pressing a tender kiss to Gwen's lips, and whispered something that made her smile grow impossibly brighter. Before he left, he winked at Tammie, a gesture so casual and charming that it warmed her cheeks despite herself.

As the door closed behind him, Tammie turned back to her sister, finding her still basking in the glow of Tristan's departure. "Isn't he amazing?" Gwen sighed, sinking further into her chair. "I can't wait for you and Niall—or whoever—to fall in love."

The bubble of warmth in Tammie's chest burst. Her earlier irritation roared back to life. "Oh, really?" she snapped, her glare sharp enough to cut glass. "It definitely will not be Niall. I thought you said a knight always keeps his word. It's been an entire day, Gwen. No Niall. No Liam. No *nada!*"

Gwen's smile vanished, replaced by a look of genuine concern. "Oh, goodness," she murmured, her hand flying to her mouth. "I hope nothing bad happened to them."

Tammie crossed her arms. "Didn't they say they'd send word if something came up? Or some sort of message?"

"It's not always possible," Gwen said, her tone quieter now, worry clouding her eyes. "If they're in Atlandia, there are places they can't just … come in and out of. That realm is awful. Worse than the North Pole."

"You've never been to the North Pole," Tammie pointed out dryly. "Unless you snuck off and went there in the past few months."

"You know what I mean," Gwen shot back, her tone impatient.

"Well, frozen wasteland or not, Niall needs to hurry up and get back. I've got an enchantment to break, and Gerard is starting to lose patience with me." Tammie threw her hands up in frustration. "I can't sit here waiting forever!"

"What did Gerard say?" Gwen asked, frowning.

"Oh, nothing much," Tammie said with mock sweetness, rolling her eyes. "Just little things like, 'How much longer until I see you again?' and 'My friends don't believe you're real.' You know, the usual."

Gwen shook her head, exasperation creeping into her voice. "Oh boy. Well, I'm sure he'll wait. From everything you've said, he's completely smitten. And Sabrina says he's a really nice guy."

Tammie huffed as she sank into the chair Tristan had vacated, her fingers tapping impatiently on the armrest. "Maybe. But if Niall doesn't get back soon, I'm going to lose my mind. And Gerard … well, let's just say his patience has its limits."

Her voice grew more resolute. "It's been nearly two

weeks since I arrived, Gwen. Another week, and I'm heading back to Georgia. Even if it's just for a couple of days."

Gwen frowned, her brows knitting together in concern. "Let's try summoning Niall," she suggested, her voice tinged with unease. "His absence is … troubling."

Tammie leaned forward, and they clasped hands tightly as they prepared for the summoning. Closing her eyes, she focused on Niall, visualizing his face, his form, his presence. At first, the image was clear, but then the edges blurred. Fog swirled through her mind, thick and suffocating, swallowing her thoughts. A dark figure emerged, its silhouette stark against the gray haze.

She tried to break free, but the figure held her captive, like invisible chains binding her mind. Pale, claw-like hands extended toward her, unnatural and menacing.

"It is time for your destiny, your truth."

The creature's voice reverberated through her, deep and resonant, chilling her to the bone. Her body began to tremble as the words soaked into her consciousness.

"No!" she gasped, her voice defiant but quivering.

"Prepare yourself. It's almost time."

"Tammie!" Gwen's urgent voice pierced the vision, hands on Tammie's shoulders shaking her back into reality. Tammie's eyes snapped open, meeting Gwen's alarmed gaze.

"What happened?" Gwen demanded, her tone filled with worry.

Tammie struggled to steady her breathing. "I … I'm not sure. Someone was in my vision—a dark, cloaked figure. It said something about preparing for my destiny."

"That sounds ... promising?" Gwen's attempted smile wavered, more nervous than reassuring.

Tammie shook her head, her unease growing. "It wasn't a good destiny, Gwen. It said something about returning to my truth. It felt almost evil."

"Your truth?" Gwen shot to her feet, pacing the room. "Should we call Mom? Maybe she knows something about this."

"Absolutely not!" Tammie stood abruptly, her expression resolute. "If we call Mom, she'll be on the next flight here, and she won't leave without dragging me back with her." She hesitated, her voice softening. "Then again ... she doesn't have to know where we're calling from. Maybe it's worth considering."

Gwen nodded thoughtfully.

"First we can try to reach Niall again." Tammie held out her hands.

"No," Gwen said firmly, already moving toward the door. "I'll check the spell book. Something feels ... off about all this."

"I'm exhausted," Tammie admitted, the weight of the vision pressing on her. "Can we deal with it in the morning?"

Gwen hesitated, then nodded. "Yes, we should wait until morning when Sabrina can join us. Leave your door open."

Tammie saluted her mockingly and retreated to her bedroom.

After a long shower, Tammie slipped into her gray fleece pajamas and climbed into bed. The warm water had washed away some of her tension, but the unsettling vision lingered. Restless, she picked up her journal, flipping through the pages. She considered her entry for the day but found herself picking up the book both Sabrina and Gwen had written notes in. Soon she was distracted by her sisters' detailed notes on the enchantment and the bizarre world they were entangled with.

It was a story straight out of a fantasy novel—suspense, adventure, passion. She almost smiled at the thought of turning it into a book one day. No one would believe it was nonfiction, but it would be a page-turner, nonetheless.

Lifting her phone, her wallpaper, a picture of her and Gerard faces pressed together, appeared on the screen. For a fleeting moment, her thoughts turned to Niall. Would he ever find love after being freed? Would he fall in love again, or was his heart still tethered to the wife he had lost?

The thought of him with someone should have been heartwarming, thinking that he could move on. But instead, it left her uneasy. Her sisters had fallen in love with the men they'd rescued. Could it happen to her, too?

A sudden image flashed in her mind: Niall, walking beside her, their hands clasped together, their gazes meeting. What would it feel like to love him under normal circumstances?

She dropped her phone with a sharp pang of guilt. How could she entertain such thoughts while staring at Gerard's picture? What was wrong with her?

Desperate to clear her mind, she pressed the call button. Gerard's voicemail picked up after a few rings, his voice cheerful and familiar.

"I am unable to answer. Leave a message."

She glanced at the time. Six in the evening. Was he on assignment? Out with friends? Tammie left a quick message and hung up, sinking back onto her pillows.

Her thoughts betrayed her once again, drifting back to Niall. What was he doing right now? Was he safe?

"Oh, God. Stop it, Tammie," she muttered, rolling onto her back.

But the question lingered in her mind. Was Niall safe? And would he ever come back?

Chapter Six

A warm breeze blew through the cottage when Tammie opened the bedroom windows. Glad she'd taken the job of keeping the guest cottages tidied, she picked up the cleaning caddie filled with sponges, cloths, and spray bottles, and went into the other room. This cottage was to be Niall's when he finally came to live here. She smiled studying the sturdy furnishings. She could see him living here.

There wasn't much to do, really, since the cottages were currently not being used. Still, the light housekeeping and airing out the four cottages made for busy work.

When the wind slammed the front door shut, she jumped and screamed. Giggling at her reaction, she went to the second bedroom to dust. She stopped short and glanced around when something brushed against her arm.

No one was there. Sure it was just the jumpiness, she ignored the feeling and began to clean.

Padriag had appeared earlier the morning after she'd tried

to last summon Niall to inform them they were now living in Atlandia, having sought asylum from attacks. He'd further explained they were not free to come and go at will but had to be granted permission by two royals.

Each time she thought about the beautiful princesses, she wanted to go see them and inform them that the men were to be rescued from there. Had Niall or Liam not explained that to them?

She considered summoning Niall, but reconsidered as she didn't want to put him in danger or get him in trouble. According to Padriag the royals had not given permission for them to leave until after they fought and defended a village. It wouldn't be good to summon him when he could be in battle, the distraction could cost him. Two weeks had passed since she'd last seen Niall, and it was much longer than she expected to have patience for.

Huffing, she ran the dusting cloth over the dark wooden surface of a dresser. Sensing a presence, she looked up into the mirror and shrieked.

It was Niall. She swung around and slapped his arm.

"You scared the crap out of me again!" Tammie yelled and hit him again. "Why can't you pop into another room and let me know you're here?"

"I can't control where I appear. I concentrate on you and come to where you are," He replied, his voice flat.

Tammie took in his appearance. His hair was longer, resting on his shoulders. He had a beard and mustache as well. Judging from the lines around his eyes and brow, the man was exhausted. His clothing was soiled and torn.

"Take your clothes off." She told him holding her hand out.

Incredulous eyes met hers. "I will not."

"You stink. I can't stand it. Go in there." Tammie pointed to the bathroom. "Take your clothes off, throw them out here. I'll wash them while you take a hot shower."

He looked toward the bathroom, longing apparent. "Hot water?"

Tammie lifted an eyebrow and smiled. "As hot as you want it. For a long while too."

Without hesitation Niall bent and pulled off his thick fur lined boots and hose. He yanked his top off and threw it on the floor next to the boots. He worked the laces to his breeches as he neared the bathroom.

Tammie could not pull her eyes away from his broad back. His skin was perfect, not one blemish or mark. The expanse of his back narrowed to a slender waist. His large biceps bulged as he flexed to remove his pants. The man had a kicking body.

He ducked into the bathroom, and she sighed. Was that disappointment she felt?

The door opened and Niall's head popped out. "Can you show me how to start the water?"

"Sure," Tammie replied wondering if he'd removed his pants. She walked straight to the shower, not looking at him. "You turn this knob here for hot water and this one for cold," she explained as she adjusted the temperature. "Stick your hand in it and tell me if that is comfortable."

Darn it. His pants were still on.

He eyed the knobs, stuck his hand under the warm water and closed his eyes. "Aye, that is fine."

"You didn't have running water in your home in the alter-world?"

"Nay, we heat water in the kitchen and took baths," he replied. She smiled to see that he kept his hand under the stream.

"Well, throw your pants out before you get in." She turned and walked out to wait.

When he finally threw the pants out, she picked up the offensive garments and carried them holding them as far from her as she could. She threw them in the washer but didn't start it, not sure if it would affect the water temperature in the shower.

She snapped her fingers at a thought and hurried back into the bathroom. Gwen had told her they'd shopped and prepared for the men's return, maybe they'd stocked clothes for Niall here. In the closet, brand new pullovers and several pair of slacks and jeans were hung. She pulled a pair of jeans off the hanger and held them up; they seemed to be the right size. There were several pair of shoes and boots lined up on the floor. A thick jacket hung besides the shirts as well as a black suit. What would Niall look like in a suit? His beautiful midnight hair and grey eyes would surely stand out.

She pulled a drawer open to find it was stocked with undershirts, briefs, boxers and socks. Would Niall be a briefs man or go commando? Soon she'd find out. She took one of each and a pair of thick socks. Then pulled a long sleeve pullover from another drawer and put all the clothing on the bed. She studied the clothing and wondered what his reaction would be.

The man was hard to figure out.

If he refused to wear the modern clothing, she'd go ahead and start the washer as soon as he finished his shower.

TAMMIE MADE two ham and cheese sandwiches along with a quick tossed salad. She heard Niall opening the bathroom door and she held her breath. He didn't make any noise, and she assumed he was dressing.

Just in case he refused to dress, she started the washer. When she turned, he stood in the kitchen, a towel wrapped around his waist. Words vanished and with her ability to think with them. She opened her mouth and then closed it.

He frowned looking past her to the washer and dryer and cocked his head to the side at the sounds coming from it. "Is my clothing ready?"

The ripples of a washboard stomach kept her gaze captive. Slowly she forced her eyes up to his well-formed pecks. Then slowly, oh so slowly, did she work herself over to the light feathering of hair between them.

Did he say something?

"Tamara Where are my clothes?"

"Oh," she a hysterical giggle escaped her. "I left clothes on the bed for you."

"I want the clothes I was wearing," he told her, lifting his hand to rake his fingers through his hair.

Biceps were not supposed to be so captivating, yet his lulled her back to muteness.

She blinked and pointed to the bedroom. "Your stinky clothes are in the washing machine, and then they will go in the dry....er the drying machine. So you'll have to stay in the towel." *Thank the lord for this gift.* "For at least an hour."

"I want them now."

"They are wet. You can't get them out, the machine locks up until it's finished." She glared at him. "Why don't you put on the clothes that I put out for you."

He glanced toward the bedroom. "No."

"What is up with you anyway," Tammie snapped, losing her temper at his stubbornness. "They are sturdier than the rags you were wearing and probably more comfortable and warmer too."

"I don't want anything from this world," he replied, glaring back. "I will wait."

"Suit yourself," Tammie told him and moved closer to him. "You're an asshole."

He remained silent, his hand moving to his towel when it slipped just a bit. Tammie bit her lip; even the anger didn't stop her from a slight pang of disappointment when it didn't fall.

"You know what your problem is Niall? You are selfish. You are so wrapped up in your bitterness that you don't care if it affects or hurts other."

The muscle in his jaw jumped. "You do not know what you speak of."

"I know that your friends love you and spend endless hours trying to figure out how to help you. They worry about you and Padriag so much that neither Tristan nor Gavin sleep well."

Tammie wanted to slap the bland expression off his face. But she continued instead. "Tell us what the terms of breaking your enchantment are. Stop being such a jerk."

"It cannot be broken. I am certain," he replied turning away from her and looking out the window.

"If you tell me what it is, then we can all brainstorm and perhaps come up with a way around it. At least give us that much." Tammie hated the pleading sound of her voice and bit back the urge to groan.

"Stop asking me to tell you. I am only here because I gave you my word I would return, nothing more." He turned to her tucking the end of his town into the top, so it stayed in place.

He actually didn't care; he wasn't going to help them. "Augh!" Fury filled her and without thinking she grabbed his arms and tried to shake him.

Niall pulled her hands off his arms and held them. His eyes widened and Tammie realized angry tears streamed down her face. She tried to pull away, but he held fast.

"Do not cry." The hoarseness in his voice caught her by surprise. His words had the reverse effect, and she began to cry harder.

"Oh shut up," she snapped between sniffs and tried to pull away, but he didn't release his hold.

"Let me go, Niall. Just forget everything. I will go back to the house and tell them you're being a selfish ass who refuses to help."

When a sob escaped her, he let out a long breath. It broke her heart to think that he doomed himself to remain alone in that other world.

"Please tell me, we'll figure out a way together," she pleaded.

"Together," he repeated the word and then shook his head. There was a tremble where he held her, it was slight, but Tammie was sure she felt it. When Niall let out a quick sharp breath, Tammie stared up at him. It was as if he fought an inner battle, his thoughts reflected in his eyes as they scanned her face. Whatever inner turmoil he fought, he seemed to be losing.

The room seemed to fade, until all she could see was him. Was he fighting the urge to tell her everything... or was it that he felt what she did. A pull tugged and her body demanded closeness between them. Tammie let out a breath, her parted lips getting his attention.

"Tell me what you want Niall." Tammie's voice trembled.

What seemed like a flicker of confusion crossed his gaze. With a deep growl he leaned forward and covered her mouth with his.

Kissed many times, Tammie was not new to the sensation of a man's lips upon hers, but never had a kiss engulfed her like Niall's did. His mouth ravished hers with an almost savage hunger. His tongue pressed her lips apart and she moaned when he began to explore her fully.

He released her hands, freeing his to travel down her back. She held on to his shoulders sure she would collapse in a heap on the floor if she let go of him.

When her legs faltered, he picked her up. Their mouths fused, he managed to carry her to the bedroom.

They tumbled onto the bed, his large body covered hers entirely, and she relished the warm hard muscles.

"I cannot stop," He murmured in short breaths into her ear. "I swear to you, I cannot stop now."

"Then don't." She turned his face to her and took his mouth again. His kisses were intoxicating. All Tammie knew was that she could not stop kissing him—did not want his lips to ever leave hers.

The sound of her sundress tearing barely registered.

"Oh God," Tammie exclaimed when his mouth moved to her breast, and he took its peak into his mouth to suckle. She raked her nails across his back arching to give him better access while tugging the towel from around him.

He moved back up to kiss her at the same time he drove his hardness into her. They both screamed at the sensation of their bodies joining. Tammie wrapped her legs around his waist urging him to move deeper.

They made love in the way of two people finding each other, of two lost lovers who never expected to be together again finally being able to touch, to kiss, to caress.

At a slow leisurely pace, as if savoring each movement, Niall took his time, his body taking hers in such an exquisite way that each moment pulled her into a place where only he and she existed. Their bodies moved in sync, giving and taking from one another, continuing on and on, the pull of falling over an edge just out of reach.

"You feel so damn good," Tammie gasped and threaded her hands through his still damp hair, pulling his face closer so she could take his lips.

The kiss deepened quickly to become almost savage, neither seeming to get enough. A flame grew and traveled up and down her body as Tammie soared higher and higher. Somehow she knew he did the same, especially when he reached under her bottom and lifted her so that he could delve deeper.

Stars burst as Tammie lost control, release slamming into her so hard she cried out. Niall lowered her onto the bed and continued the wonderful assault of her body, his husky moans so breathtakingly sensual. Finally, he trembled, letting go.

Niall collapsed over her, his harsh breaths in her ear. Tammie wrapped her arms around his waist, holding him tightly against her, not wanting to lose the connection.

She felt a strong sense that a tie had formed between them. A bond that would not be easily broken.

The cottage was silent, the only sounds were their breathing and the wind outside. Tammie dared not speak, afraid of breaking the spell of the moment.

Niall on the other hand had a different point of view. He thrust himself away from her. Dark, tormented eyes met hers.

"What have I done?" He grabbed the stack of clothes off the bed and practically ran into the bathroom slamming the door behind him.

"Niall, don't be an idiot!" Tammie screamed after him. "Come back here and talk to me."

The sound of him moving in the bathroom was her only reply. She jumped from the bed and pounded on the door. "Damn it Niall, open the fucking door."

"So much for afterglow." Tammie grumbled, going to the dresser to grab a T-shirt since her dress was ruined.

"You can't stay in there forever," she told the closed door.

He could dematerialize. "Niall? Don't forget you gave me your word, you'd help free Padriag."

A thump told he was still in the bathroom.

She walked out of the bedroom without a clear destination in mind, just knowing she needed to clear her head.

The brightness of the kitchen made her come to a stop, and Tammie covered her face with her hands.

"Oh my god." Her body hummed from Niall's touch, it was so strange, how it had felt as if it recognized him. She let out a long breath.

What had she just done?

She'd cheated on her boyfriend. "Oh my god." Tammie covered her face with both hands. "I am a cheater. A ho."

First thing, after Niall left, she would call Gerard and confess. Or maybe not confess and just break things off. She'd never done something like this before. What was she supposed to do?

Guilt should have overshadowed everything, but she couldn't keep from looking to the doorway.

Chapter Seven

Niall pulled on the soft blue pants, their unfamiliar texture feeling strange against his skin. He'd seen Padriag wear something similar and heard him call them *jeans*. The name was odd, but the material had a certain sturdiness to it that surprised him. Perhaps they were better suited for riding or battle than his trusted breeches. He ran his fingers over the fabric, marveling at its resilience, and yet, despite their practicality, a part of him still felt unsettled in these strange clothes, in this modern world.

The cottage was silent beyond the door, an oppressive stillness that gnawed at him. Was Tamara still there? Her angry voice echoed in his mind, the memory of her pounding on the bathroom door. She'd had every right to be furious. His behavior had been unpardonable, and he knew it.

A groan escaped his lips, low and filled with regret, as he sank onto the edge of the bed, his head dropping into his hands. What had he done? The weight of his actions was a crushing burden, the consequences too terrible to truly consider. He had always prided himself on his control, his discipline. And yet, with Tamara, something had overtaken him—a force so powerful, so overwhelming, that it had shattered the walls he'd spent centuries building.

It wasn't just desire. It was something deeper, a recognition. A pull of two souls that had somehow found their way to each other after lifetimes apart. He had been helpless against it, as had she. And now, they were both ensnared in a dangerous web.

Niall's gaze shifted to the door. He couldn't leave things as they were. He had to find Tamara and apologize, though words felt woefully inadequate. He hadn't been a gentleman in any sense of the word. Worse still, he'd hidden from her— not out of cowardice, but because he'd realized too late the danger he'd placed her in.

Devina.

Her name was a curse in his mind. The demon had warned him, time and again, of the consequences if he ever lay with another woman. She would destroy anyone who dared to touch his heart. He'd thought himself immune, his heart encased in ice too thick for anyone to penetrate. But Tamara had melted it with a single glance, and now her life was in peril if Devina discovered the truth.

He stood, his resolve hardening. At the foot of the bed, a shirt lay folded neatly beside a pair of boots. He picked it up —soft and warm, unlike the rough tunics of his past. Everything fit him perfectly, as if prepared with care. A pang of guilt twisted in his chest. Tamara had thought of everything, even when he'd refused her kindness.

Despite her fiery temper, she was kind, caring and, by the way she'd continued to try to help him, patient. She'd cried when he refused to reveal the terms of his enchantment, her tears undoing him in ways he couldn't explain. And the way she'd looked at him ... the heat in her gaze had stirred a fire in him that had long been extinguished. When he'd held her, he'd felt the warmth of her body pressed against his, all his carefully guarded control had shattered.

With the boots on, he could delay no longer. He stepped out of the room, his chest tightening at the sight before him.

Tamara sat curled in a large chair, her legs pulled to her chest, her chin resting on her knees. She'd tugged the oversized white item she wore over her legs, but it did little to hide the rose-colored undergarments beneath. She looked fragile, and yet there was a stubborn defiance in the way she glared at him, her dark eyes flashing with anger.

The sight of her, so alluring and fierce, made his breath catch. He took a step closer, then hesitated as her frown deepened.

"I apologize," he began, his voice low and rough.

"Don't." She raised a hand, her palm facing him. "Don't you *dare* apologize for what happened between us. If you're going to apologize, do it for what you did afterward."

Her words were a challenge, her gaze daring him to argue. She wasn't going to make this easy.

"I apologize for leaving the bed so abruptly," he said after a moment. "It was not a gentlemanly thing to do."

Her eyes narrowed. "And?"

His brows furrowed. What else was she expecting? He

tried again. "I should not have been ungrateful for the clothing."

Tamara's gaze flicked over him, taking in his jeans and shirt as if noticing them for the first time. Heat rose to his face as her eyes lingered, the weight of her scrutiny igniting something deep within him. With a delicate shrug, she sniffed and looked back up. "Everything fits."

"Aye, it does."

Again, she rested her cheek on her knees, her lashes lowering to hide her expression. "I'm not going to ask about your enchantment. I don't have the energy to argue with you anymore."

Her quiet resignation pierced him. Guilt twisted like a knife in his chest, and he dropped his gaze to the floor. If only he could tell her the truth—the real reason why he could never be free.

Devina's hold was an unbreakable chain, the enchantment's terms cruel and unyielding. To break it would demand a sacrifice so great, he couldn't bear to ask it of anyone, least of all Tamara.

The sudden pull toward the alter-world jolted him, his body tensing instinctively. He turned to her, his heart heavy. "I must go."

Her eyes widened, wariness shadowing her face. "Will you return?"

The question was simple, but the vulnerability in her voice struck him like a blow. He didn't want to feel anything for her, but the urge to go to her, to pull her into his arms and promise her the world, was overwhelming.

"Aye," he said softly. "I will return. Padriag must be freed."

For a moment, their eyes met, and he almost fought the pull, almost stayed. But the image of Atlandia burned in his mind, a cruel reminder of his reality.

With a heavy heart, Niall surrendered to the magic and disappeared.

CHAPTER EIGHT

The kingdom had two kinds of warriors, sentinels, whose main form was as a wolf and shifters, who remained in human form mostly. Along with Atlandia's mounted warriors—most of whom were also shifters—Niall and Padriag held back as the battle against Meliot's forces began. As soon as the black wolves descended over a hill, Atlandia's sentinels sprang forward with so much speed it was a blur as they charged. The sounds of snarls and howls filled the air as the shifters and wolves fought.

Niall did his best to keep up with what transpired, but it was hard to tell as the wolves and shifters moved at supernatural speeds. It seemed Atlandia's wolves were larger and were winning so far.

Deep growls sounded as mounted armored horsemen came into view. Niall looked to his left, where Argo sat upon a huge warhorse. All the horses wore magically warded plates around their breast, sides and legs. The animals pawed the ground and grunted, filling the cold air with the steam of their breath. It seemed they were anxious to enter the fight.

"Arms!" Argo called out and swords were yanked from scabbards, mines swung in the air and lances fell forward. Niall held his longsword in his right hand, leaving his other weaponry on his body. Daggers were strapped across his armored chest, a short sword at his right hip and a claymore on his left.

The pounding of the horses' hooves on the ground was like thunder as they rode through the tangle of wolves still battling and on toward Meliot's soulless warriors. One last glance to ensure Padriag was next to him was reassuring. An excellent archer, Liam had been recruited to the archery group and remained behind with the archers.

Battle was one of the few times Niall was grateful for being a warrior in his past life in the other realm. With a wide swing, his longsword sent several of Meliot's warriors flying from their perches and onto the ground, deep cuts through their mid sections. Within moments, the enemy fighters gave him wide berth, hoping he'd be taken down by an arrow.

Not relenting, he turned his horse around and charged to where Padriag fought. While the young knight fought one opponent, another came from behind. The fighter screamed in pain at an unexpected strike across his waist and back. Niall followed the hit with a second blow, his blade cutting the fighter's head off.

Padriag's sword plunged into his opponent's stomach and the warrior fell from his steed onto the now bloody ground.

"I had it all under control," Padriag called out, frowning

at Niall. "I knew that guy was behind me. I was ready with my Ninja moves."

"What about him?" Niall motioned with his head as a warrior charged toward Padriag, a sharp lance dangerously close.

Letting out a long breath, Padriag flung his left hand toward the lance-carrying man, sending him flying through the air until landing atop several wolves, who then attacked him.

"If you can use your magic, why are you not?" Niall yelled as he dispatched another opponent. "You are an idiot."

"Not as fun," Padriag yelled back.

Although both forces were about evenly matched, Niall wasn't sure who was besting the other side. As the fight continued, arrows flew, hitting both bands of warriors.

"Do something," Niall called out, glaring at Padriag.

"It won't be a fair fight," Padriag waved his hands as if directing music and yelled out words that sounded like gibberish. Instantly, the arrow seemed to stop midair and fell to the ground, neither side able to penetrate the invisible barrier.

Padriag directed his horse towards Niall. Both fought off opponents and the younger man blew out a breath. "Unfortunately the shield blocks arrows from all sides, but it's better than nothing. I don't want to get pierced through when I'm about to get freed."

Without looking, Padriag yanked a dagger from his belt and flung it over his shoulder, the blade impaled a warrior charging toward him right between the eyes. "I don't wanna look," Padriag said with a mock shiver. "Is it bad?"

Niall ignored him.

It wasn't much longer before it was apparent that Atlandia's forces were winning the battle. Meliot's warriors retreated, leaving behind the dead and injured.

Niall was finally able to sag with exhaustion, his entire body wet with sweat and blood. He'd not kept count of how many he'd killed. Considering the lack of blood on some of the fallen, most of Meliot's warriors weren't human.

Liam rushed toward him and Padriag, his gaze moving over them. "Are either of you injured?"

It took a moment for Niall to assess himself. As far as he could tell, none of the blood was his. After flexing both arms and running hands over his torso, he was satisfied he was uninjured.

"I think I broke something," Padriag said. He held up his left hand to show the two outer fingers were bent unnaturally. "Ouch."

Liam tore a strip of fabric from the hem of Padriag's shirt and, after straightening the broken fingers whilst Padriag gritted his teeth, he bound them together and tied them to the other two to keep them immobile.

The warriors began inventory of the dead and wounded, the latter being loaded onto wagons to be brought to healers. As night came, the human warriors hurried toward the safety of the castle to avoid the impending icing.

UPON REACHING the safety of the castle, the men's clothing was removed by servants, and they were directed to the bathing rooms. It was like a cave. Water streamed from shallow trenches that stuck out from the walls into two large bathing pools. From one wall, cylinders protruded spouting water onto the wet stone floor.

Niall went directly to one of the cylinders, deciding he didn't want to bathe in water filled with men who were covered in blood and other unrecognizable things. It seemed most had the same idea as soon lines formed at the waterfalls.

As the tepid water washed away the battle soil, Niall closed his eyes, allowing the falling water to massage his battered body.

Once satisfied he was clean, he accepted a drying cloth from a servant and went to find fresh clothes.

After a hearty meal and plenty of ale, Niall could barely keep his eyes open. He prayed for a reprise from Devina, as he knew it would be impossible to stay awake.

THE FAMILIAR DAMPNESS of the dungeon crept through Niall's clothing, the icy moisture clinging to his skin like a second layer. The fetid stench of rot and decay curled into his nostrils, forcing him to gag. Blind in the oppressive darkness, he groped his way toward the rough stone wall, leaning against its cold surface to steady himself.

An uneasy stillness hung in the air, unnatural and foreboding. Devina's guards were usually swift, their heavy footsteps echoing before they even reached him. But now, only silence answered. His heart pounded in the hollow of his chest, each beat bringing rising dread.

A faint shuffle broke the quiet. Niall froze, his senses

straining toward the sound. Torchlight flickered ahead, throwing grotesque shadows across the damp cell walls.

"She's nae here," a gravelly voice rumbled from the darkness, rough and callous. The figure holding the torch stepped closer, revealing a hulking, rotund man with bleary eyes and a cruel smile. "I donna ken when she'll return."

"Then why am I here?" Niall demanded, his voice steady despite the threat before him.

The guard sneered, stepping closer to the bars. His grimy fingers curled around a whip hanging from his belt, its straps ending in jagged, rusted hooks. "I suppose I can still torture ye. Devina's nae here to stop me."

"She must be near, else I wouldn't be here," Niall said sharply, his gaze unwavering.

The man chuckled, a low, malevolent sound. "Did ye nae hear me? She left." He began to unlock the cell door with deliberate slowness, savoring Niall's tension.

Niall edged closer to the door, weighing his options. He could outrun the heavy man—if the opportunity arose. But before he could act, another guard appeared, tall and wiry, his expression grim.

"Our Mistress has returned and wishes to speak to him first," the newcomer said, his tone clipped. He shoved the door open, gesturing for Niall to follow.

As Niall stepped out, the hulking guard grinned, revealing rotting teeth. "Aye, I'll be here waitin' for ye." He hefted the whip, letting the cruel hooks dangle menacingly.

The guard escorted Niall to a room that was blindingly bright, the stark contrast to the dungeon almost disorienting.

The whitewashed walls gleamed with a false purity, and carefully curated illusions.

Devina stood by a massive window, her silhouette framed against an ocean view he knew was fabricated. Everything about her was deliberate: the thin linen dress clinging to her curves, the way the light danced around her, the coy tilt of her head as she turned to face him. Her beauty was a weapon, as calculated as the cruelty she wielded.

"You haven't slept," she said, her tone laced with amusement. "Do you really think staying awake keeps me away from you?"

Niall kept his gaze fixed beyond her, refusing to engage.

"Tell me," she murmured, stepping closer, her voice like poisoned honey. "Did you not miss me? You belong to me and only me."

She circled him, her fingers grazing his shoulder, sending an icy dread down his spine. She leaned in, her breath warm against his ear. "We should have a child, Niall. What do you think about that? An offspring, a product of our joining. Will that make you happy?"

Niall's jaw tightened, his hatred for her burning brighter than his fear. This was his nightmare—to be trapped here, to have the others above believe him dead, to be buried alive in this cursed realm with her forever.

"You tensed," Devina observed, her lips curling into a cruel smile. "The thought terrifies you, doesn't it?" She moved in front of him, her gaze locking on his. "But you'll join me in bed. And—" Her words cut off, and her nostrils flared. She leaned closer, sniffed. and without warning, she slapped him hard across the face. When he didn't react, she splayed her fingers, palm in his direction sending a burst of energy that felt like a huge boulder flattening his face.

"You bastard!" she shrieked.

Warm blood trickled down his chin from his nose and split lip. Niall remained still. His lack of emotion was not something he had to force, because in reality, he'd stopped caring what she did. For a long time, he'd lost the ability to fear death or suffering.

"You fucked someone. Do not try to deny it," she hissed, her voice venomous. "I will find her and when I do, you will watch as I torture her."

When he didn't respond, Devina hit Niall again, her fury unbridled.

Devina let out an unhuman screech, her eyes burned red, and her dress transformed into a murky gray, hanging limp on her now much thinner body.

Despite seeing her react to the many times he'd rejected her, this time her transformation was shocking. Niall took a step backward. What stood before him was a demon, there was no doubt in his mind. The being stretched until about a foot taller than him, and Devina's face sunk into the bones of a skull that was elongated, long teeth filling the gap of its mouth. Long skinny arms hung down past its knees, the long talons at the tips almost touching the floor. Feet like hooves and a hunched back made for a terrifying sight.

Devina turned away for a moment, seeming almost as if not expecting to have shown her true form. Then screeching again, the sound like that of many voices, Devina whirled to face him. "You will pay."

The guards rushed into the room their heads swiveling between the demon and Niall.

"Take him," she commanded, her now deep voice dripping with malevolence. "Beat him until he passes out. Then wake him and start again."

When the guards grabbed his arms, Devina neared and grabbed his face, the long talon nails digging into his skin. "One chance to save her life," she whispered. "Give yourself to me, body and soul. Remain here in this realm away from Meliot, away from the useless games he forces you to play. Be mine."

"Never," Niall spat, his voice cold as steel.

The demon's eyes closed slowly, then opened, staring directly into his. "Then you will suffer."

IN THE DUNGEON, they chained him to a post, the rusted iron biting into his wrists. The hate he'd felt in Devina's presence grew deeper, soon replaced by a seething rage he couldn't unleash. The first lash tore into his back, the hooks rending flesh and leaving behind searing trails of agony.

He gritted his teeth, refusing to scream, waiting for the sweet release of darkness to claim him.

Suddenly, he wasn't in the dungeon any longer. Instead, Niall lay on a soft blanket, the sun warming him.

At the sound of waves crashing against the shore, he inhaled the salty air, refusing to open his eyes and face reality. No doubt another trick of Devina's.

"Da are ye asleep?" The sweet voice caused him to jerk to a sitting position.

"Maribel, leave your Da alone," Caitlin called from nearby, holding his younger daughter Beatrice's hand. A seashell glinted between the chubby fingers of the child's other hand.

"Da!" Beatrice called out with a giggle.

Struck speechless, he watched the scene before him. It was the summer. He and his wife had taken the girls to the seashore for the day. He never forgot the day, the last time he'd spent time alone with his family.

The wind blew Caitlin's skirts flush against her and her large stomach became obvious. She was expecting their third child. His son.

"Here, love, come to me." His wife spread her arms calling Maribel to her. The four-year-old ran to her giggling. Niall tried to focus on Caitlin's face. It was blurry, and he blinked and squinted trying to see her clearly. But the sun shone too brightly behind her, and he couldn't make her features out.

"Go back to sleep Niall, rest." Caitlin's voice was like a whisper in the breeze.

"No!" He screamed, but their faces grew fainter. He scrambled to his feet and ran toward them.

The scene faded and he fell to his knees.

NIALL WAS ONCE AGAIN in Devina's opulent bedroom, his body trembling with emotion and pain. He wasn't sure what had occurred. The room shimmered with unnatural light, the air heavy with the scent of perfumed oils and something darker, more sinister. As always, his injuries were mysteriously gone—no bruises, no open wounds, no scars from the whip's cruel hooks. But the phantom pain lingered, burrowing deep into his bones, a constant reminder of her torment.

"Lay with me," Devina, back in her familiar form, circled him, her voice seductive but laced with evil at the same time.

"Never," he rasped, his voice a broken growl.

"You will." Her words, deceptively soft, carried the weight of a command. She flung her arm toward him, and an invisible force slammed into his chest. Niall flew through the air, colliding with the stone wall so hard it jolted the breath from his lungs. He crumpled to the floor, his weakened body collapsing under the impact.

Her laughter was cruel, echoing in the room, many voices at once. With a flick of her wrist, her dark magic seized him again, lifting him effortlessly and flinging him onto the bed. The silken sheets, cool and deceptive in their softness, mocked. He twisted, trying to roll off, but before he could move, straps of leather slithered around his ankles and wrists, binding him to the bed.

He struggled, his muscles straining, but the bindings didn't budge. His strength, already depleted, diminished further with every futile tug. His head fell back against the pillows, and a guttural howl escaped his throat—raw, primal, and desperate.

"Do it, Niall. Accept me as your master," Devina purred, standing over him like a queen triumphant. Her black eyes glinted with malice as her lips curled into a smile. "Or tonight, she dies."

Her hands fell on him, caressing his chest and shoulders, their touch meant to seduce but only igniting disgust within him. Her fingers trailed down his torso, each movement calculated, each brush of her skin a cruel mockery of affection.

This time, though, he didn't flinch. He didn't give her the satisfaction. The fury he'd held back for so long erupted, his body trembling with its intensity.

"It matters not what you do. I will nae be yours," he roared, the word carrying every ounce of defiance he could muster.

Devina straddled him, her nails digging into his shoulders as she leaned closer. "Don't fight me," she hissed, her breath hot against his ear. "You know you will never win." Her lips pressed against his neck, her kisses like venom seeping into his skin.

Then, something shifted. The straps binding him snapped with a sudden, violent force. Before Devina could react, Niall surged upward, throwing her off him. She tumbled backward, hitting the floor with a cry of surprise. An ornate bedside table flew across to where she was and crashed beside her, its contents scattering across the polished stone.

Her face twisted with rage as she scrambled to her feet. With a snarl, she lunged toward him again. But an invisible barrier sprang up between them, shimmering faintly in the dim light. She slammed into it and stumbled back, her fists pounding uselessly against the clear, unyielding wall.

"Who is this witch?" she screamed, her voice shrill and

full of rage. Her eyes darted around the room, wild with fury. "Who dares enter my private quarters?"

Niall, still slumped on the floor beside the bed, stared at her in confusion. His body was heavy, drained of energy, but a warmth began to flow through him—gentle, soothing, and unmistakably familiar. It wrapped around him like a cloak, healing the invisible wounds Devina's torture had left behind. He took a deep, shuddering breath, his body filling with strength again.

Wake up, Niall. The voice was soft yet commanding, a whisper in his mind. Tamara's voice.

"I can't," he groaned, fighting against a strong lull to remain asleep, in Devina's realm.

Yes, you can. Wake up. Now.

With a sudden gasp, Niall's eyes flew open. A golden light filtered through a window onto his bed, the high ceiling greeted him, and the chill of the dungeon was replaced by the bedchamber he shared with his friends.

He was back. Safe.

"First meal is being served. I'm going down." Liam's voice cut through the haze.

Padriag stood just outside the bathroom, his expression curious. "Whoa, Niall, you look ... different. Got some good sleep, eh?" the young man continued. "You coming?"

Niall stretched, his muscles surprisingly loose, his body renewed. "Aye, I am."

As he rose to his feet, the weight of being in Devina's realm seemed to slip away, replaced by a renewed and strange lightness.

He looked at Padriag, his voice steady. "As soon as the meal is over, I'm going to the other realm. Are you?"

Padraig grinned. "Sure, I'll come along."

For the first time in what felt like years, Niall allowed himself a faint smile. A sense of purpose was returning, and with it, hope.

CHAPTER NINE

Tammie paced along the edge of the castle gardens, her long skirts swirling around her legs with each hurried step, the hem of fabric brushing her ankles. The crisp morning air nipped at her cheeks despite the bright sunshine filtering through the shedding branches overhead. She clutched her cardigan tighter, her arms crossed against the chill.

"You look pensive," Sabrina's voice broke through the silence as walked toward Tammie, a cup of coffee in each hand. Offering one to Tammie, she said. "What's going on little Tammie?"

"I had ... a dream last night," Tammie said, her voice low and uncertain. She turned her gaze upward, scanning the pale sky as if searching for answers. "Except, it didn't feel like a dream. It was too vivid. Too real."

Sabrina's brows furrowed with interest as she sank onto a nearby bench, the wood creaking beneath her. "What happened? Tell me everything."

Tammie took a sip of her coffee, the creamy richness grounding her momentarily. "I was somewhere else," she began, her voice unsteady. "With Niall. I could see him, but I wasn't really *there*. I couldn't touch anything or make myself seen." Her voice cracked as her hands tightened around the cup. "Sabrina, he was being tortured. These ... creatures, horrible and inhuman, were whipping him. He was in so much pain."

Sabrina's expression turned grave. "Niall? Tortured? What kind of creatures?"

"I don't know what they were," Tammie said, her words trembling. "But it doesn't stop there. One moment he was being flogged, and then ... the next, he was in a bed with a woman."

Sabrina froze, her cup halfway to her lips. "A woman?"

"She looked like one," Tammie clarified, her tone darkening. "But there was something wrong about her. An aura—black, heavy. She felt ... demonic, evil."

The memory clawed at Tammie's mind as she sat on a wooden bench beside Sabrina, her cup clutched with both hands. "She was demanding that he give himself to her. When he refused. She tied him to the bed, and I think—" Her voice faltered, but the implication hung heavy between them.

Sabrina's hand flew to her mouth. "Oh my God, Tammie. Are you sure it wasn't just a nightmare?"

"I don't know." Tammie shook her head, her dark eyes clouded with doubt. "But it felt so real. I could feel her wickedness, her intent. And then, somehow, I pushed her away—not with my hands, but with my mind. I just *willed* her to leave him alone."

Sabrina's eyes widened. "You *fought* her?"

"Yes." Tammie exhaled shakily. "Then somehow I realized she had control over him because he was sleeping. I screamed at him to wake up. The moment I did, he vanished."

Sabrina set her cup down, her fingers knitting together as she searched Tammie's face. "Do you think this has something to do with the other vision you had? The one about the claws clutching Niall?"

Tammie nodded slowly, her thoughts tumbling over one another. "It has to. This isn't just my imagination. Something is after him, Sabrina. And it felt as if it's been going on for a long time."

The two women sat in silence, the weight of Tammie's revelation settling like a shadow over the garden, the cool air suddenly feeling much colder.

"Come inside. We need to discuss this with Gwen," Sabrina urged, her voice firm but not overbearing.

"Give me a few minutes. I need to clear my head," Tammie replied, relieved when her sister didn't press further.

As Sabrina stood and walked away, Tammie inhaled and exhaled slowly. The crisp air felt great in her lungs. The quiet surrounding her felt as if the world were holding its breath. What troubled her most wasn't the lingering fear she'd felt after attacking a demon, but the startling surge of power she'd unleashed. She hadn't known she was capable of anything like that. It had taken immense strength—strength she'd never even attempted or knew she had. All her life, she'd accepted that Sabrina and Gwen were the gifted ones, their abilities far stronger than hers. That truth had never bothered Tammie. She actually preferred to stand at the edges of their metaphysical world.

But the night before had shifted something within her. Funny how a single night could topple everything you thought you knew about yourself.

Her phone buzzed, breaking through the tangle of thoughts. Glancing down, she saw Gerard's name on the screen, and guilt knotted her stomach. The message was curt, short.

"Dropped off your stuff at your apartment. Left the key on the kitchen table."

A fresh wave of regret washed over her. She'd already apologized—profusely, tearfully—when she confessed her betrayal, but Gerard hadn't lashed out. He hadn't even raised his voice. Instead, there had been a chilling calm in his response, as though he'd been waiting for her to end things. His quiet acceptance hurt more than any angry words could have. She remembered the long silence after her confession, the way her heart pounded until she finally asked, "Are you still there?"

He'd answered simply, without emotion. "I figured this would happen sooner or later."

After hanging up, she'd immediately reached out to a mutual friend, desperate for reassurance that Gerard was all right. The next day, she'd received a brief text stating he was bummed but moving on. Somehow, it made her feel only marginally less terrible.

Tammie slipped her phone back into the deep pocket of

her sweater making it hang lower on one side. She tracked Sabrina's slow, deliberate steps as her sister meandered back toward the front of the castle.

How had her life become so complicated, so quickly? And what was she supposed to do with this new, unsettling power that now seemed to pulse just beneath her skin?

One thing was certain—nothing would ever be the same again.

***

WHEN NIALL APPEARED in modern-day Scotland, the chill in the air struck him first, sharp and bracing. He found himself outdoors, standing amidst a garden bursting with late blooms and thick greenery. The scent of damp earth and pine filled his nostrils, grounding him in a place that was both familiar and foreign. As he turned toward the imposing stone structure before him, recognition clicked into place—it was the McRainey castle. Tristan's home.

Clouds churned overhead, casting a silvery-gray hue over the landscape, while a brisk wind tugged at his clothes and ruffled his hair. The weight of being back on the land where he had been born pressed down on him, stirring emotions he didn't want to acknowledge. He steeled himself against the rush of sentiment, forcing his thoughts to remain neutral as he surveyed the grounds.

The land was lush, vibrant green stretching in every direction. Stables stood proudly to the east, their timber frames sturdy against the elements, while meandering paths cut through the grounds, leading toward the castle or to a handful of nearby cottages. The scene was picturesque, yet it carried an air of unease—as if the land itself sensed his inner turmoil.

A sudden tingle traveled up his legs and arms, a strange, almost charged sensation that made him tense. He turned just as Tamara appeared from the side of the castle. Her skirts swirled around her ankles as she moved, the bright colors of her flowing garments melding into the lush landscape. Her eyes locked onto him, sharp and assessing, and the corners of her lips twitched when she took in his modern attire. Jeans and a gray pullover—terms Padriag had insisted he learn, though they still felt foreign on his tongue.

Tamara hurried toward him, concern etched in her expression. "How are you?" she asked, her voice low but urgent. Her eyes flicked over his face, searching for any sign of injury. "Are you hurt?"

Niall shook his head, his tone calm, though pride edged his words. "I am unharmed. The battle was not long."

Her brows shot up, and her mouth fell open in shock. "Battle? What battle?"

"We fought against Meliot's army. Our side won." His lips curved in a faint, satisfied smile. "They were barely a threat. Is Padriag here?"

She studied him for a moment, her gaze narrowing as though trying to decipher his mood. "He's inside. Told me you were to come as well. When you didn't appear in the library or in my room, I was going to check the cottage." A faint pink crept across her cheeks,

Her blush deepened, and Niall suspected her thoughts mirrored his own, replaying the last time they'd been together in this realm. An awkward silence settled between them, though it wasn't uncomfortable.

Finally breaking the quiet, Niall glanced at her sideways. "I expected you would have returned home."

Tamara's chin lifted, her eyes steady and resolute. "There's no reason for me to return. I'm staying as long as I have to, to ensure you and Padriag are freed." Her voice carried a steely determination, cutting through any argument he might have made. "What have you decided, Niall? Will you help us, or will you keep silent and leave yourself—and Padriag—trapped?"

Did it mean she was no longer in a relationship? Niall remained stubbornly silent. From the corner of his eye, he saw her tilt her head slightly, studying him as though he were an intricate puzzle she was trying to solve.

Tamara sighed, and her shoulders sagged as she turned her gaze upward. For a few moments, she stared at the swirling clouds, lost in thought. He followed her line of sight, letting the cool breeze wash over his face. It carried with it a familiar scent he had missed—the fresh, clean air of Scotland, unlike anything in the otherworld.

"Niall," she said softly, her voice almost carried away by the wind. "Your decision to stay in the alter-world affects everyone in this house. None of the men can truly live their lives while you and Padriag remain trapped under Meliot's enchantment. Do you understand how gutted they are? Imagine how you would feel if they were trapped, and you were free."

He clenched his jaw, refusing to respond. Her words hit too close to the mark, and he wasn't ready to admit how much his choice had cost not just himself but everyone around him.

When he didn't reply, she took a step closer, frustration flashing in her eyes. Without warning, she leaned in and jabbed a finger into his chest. The unexpected contact sent a jolt through him, and he stiffened under her touch.

"My sisters say neither Tristan nor Gavin are at ease. They constantly worry, knowing it's just you and Padriag trapped and having to be pulled into Meliot's dangerous games."

"It's their choice to be affected by my decision," he said tersely, though his voice lacked conviction.

At her sharp intake of breath, he braced himself for the next onslaught. She wasn't going to let this go—and for some reason, he wasn't sure he wanted her to.

Tammie blew air up at her hair and it flopped back across her brow. Her clear blue eyes flickered over him. She took her time studying him and he shifted, unsure what she looked for.

Her upper teeth pressed into her bottom lip as she met his gaze. "You know, if you decided to come back to this realm, you could make your living as a physical trainer. "

"Trainer?" Niall frowned, not sure about her sudden change of subject.

"You are muscular and well defined. Men would kill to have your physique ... er body type. Women definitely desire for men to look like you."

He scowled at her sudden change of subject and looked down to study his body, then he shrugged. "People in this time are not content with what they look like?"

This time, her rich laughter rang out loudly and his lips ached to curve into a smile. Watching her cover her mouth in mirth, he wondered what he'd said that was so funny. "Oh if you only knew. You will find out soon enough."

He followed her into a garden or perhaps a small courtyard, surrounded on three sides by a waist-high stone crafted wall.

Gavin strode out into the courtyard, sunlight glinting off his golden skin, each muscle taut beneath the fabric of his thick shirt. His gaze met Niall's for the briefest of moments —sharp, guarded—before he passed by without a word. He leaned against the stone wall, folding his arms across his broad chest, his stance radiating tension.

"Are you going to tell her the terms of breaking your enchantment or not?" Gavin's voice was low but edged with frustration. A sudden, unexpected and unwelcome pang of guilt twisted in Niall's chest.

"It matters not," Niall replied, his tone as hard. "It is impossible to break. No one—unless mad—would ever agree to try."

"There are ways around Meliot's enchantments." Gavin's slight smile was the kind that never quite reached his eyes. "Take mine, for instance. I couldn't bear a woman's touch, which made my terms seem impossible—my Sabrina had to make love to me to break it. Seemed insurmountable, didn't it? And yet ..." He trailed off, the silence serving as its own explanation.

Niall stiffened, standing straighter. The conversation stirred something he didn't want to confront. "I have to go.

Can you help Tamara understand that all of you need to concentrate on finding a way to help Padriag?"

"No, he can't," Tamara interrupted, her voice cutting through the air, tight with irritation. "I need to ask you a couple more questions before you poof out of here."

Niall turned to Gavin, who merely shrugged, the faintest smirk tugging at his lips before he pushed off the wall and walked away, leaving Niall alone with her. He sighed inwardly, bracing himself for whatever was coming.

Painfully transparent doubt clouded Tamara's gaze, frustration knit her brow, and uncertainty flickered in the way she shuffled her feet. She bit her bottom lip in thought, her eyes locked on his as though willing him to answer the question she hadn't yet voiced. The intensity of her emotions hit him like a wave, raw and unfiltered.

"Before you go, I want to ask you a favor," she said, her voice soft but unwavering. She took a tentative step closer. "Can you ... give me a hug?"

The request jolted him, knocking the breath from his lungs. A hug? Of all things? He hadn't hugged anyone since his wife. The memory was a ghostly ache he kept buried deep, and now it threatened to resurface.

Before he could respond, she closed the distance between them, slipping her arms around his waist and resting her head against his chest. Her warmth seeped into him, soft and unexpected, cutting through the cold armor he'd worn for so long.

His body froze, unyielding at first. He told himself not to move, but something within him betrayed that command. Slowly, almost unwillingly, his arms lifted and wrapped around her. His chin rested atop her head, her hair brushing against his jaw. He closed his eyes, the scent of her—wildflowers and something sweet—filling his senses, anchoring him to the moment.

"I want to help you, Niall," she whispered, her voice muffled against his chest. "But at the same time, I want what's best for you. It's not fair for us to place this burden on you. I'm so sorry." Her words ended with a soft sniff, the sound fragile, breaking through his defenses. Something inside him cracked. He found himself wanting to promise her anything, anything at all, just to keep her from crying again.

Abruptly, he pulled back, breaking the contact before he could lose himself in it completely. As he stepped away, a strange, almost dizzying sensation swept over him, as if life had been breathed back into him after years of numbness. His heart pounded in his chest, not from fear or battle, but from something far more overwhelming. Hope. It filled him, light and heady, threatening to spill over.

"I will disclose the terms of breaking my enchantment," he said suddenly, his voice steadier than he felt. "Only so that you understand the impossibility of it—and so you'll stop asking."

Tamara's eyes widened, a mixture of shock and curiosity flashing across her face. "I'm listening."

"Do not worry, Tamara," Niall added, his gaze softening despite the weight of his words. "I am sure you and the others will find a way to free Padriag ... and leave me behind."

His thoughts tumbled one over the other. He was not ready for this. Not in the slightest.

. . .

TAMMIE HELD HER BREATH, anxiety crackling through her like static as a dozen grim scenarios flickered in her mind. She clutched her hands tightly, waiting for Niall to explain the terms of breaking the enchantment that had held him prisoner in an alternate world for three centuries.

Her gaze flicked to him, searching for some sign of reassurance. Instead, she found his stormy grey eyes watching her with the same trepidation she felt. He looked every bit a man bearing the weight of a lifetime's worth of sorrow. After all, he'd lost his family, his life, his world. And here she was—worrying about how this would affect her.

"Okay," she said, forcing her voice to steady. "I'm ready. Just tell me what ridiculous thing that stupid wizard put in your enchantment to make it so hard to break."

Niall swallowed hard. The silence stretched between them, heavy and fraught. His hesitation made her pulse race. Whatever he was about to reveal clearly cost him to even put into words.

Finally, he dragged a hand over his face and shifted his gaze to the distant horizon, as if searching for strength out there in the fading light. "When I left, my wife, Caitlin, was about six months along in her pregnancy." His voice grew quieter, tinged with sadness. "He would have been our first son. We already had two little girls."

He paused, the tension radiating from him palpable. "My family was my whole world. For the first years of the enchantment, nothing mattered to me, except getting back to them. When I lost them, I lost everything."

Tammie blinked rapidly, willing back the sting of tears. "I'm so sorry, Niall. Were you ... were you ever able to go back? To visit them?"

His throat worked, the struggle evident in the way he spoke. "Twice," he said, voice rough with memory. "The first time, I learned Caitlin had given birth to a healthy boy. She named him after me." His lips twitched, a flicker of a smile cutting through the grief. "Loud, strong cry, he had." He shook his head as though dismissing the thought.

"The second time I was able to return, it was different. Caitlin had remarried. My children—" His voice cracked, his gaze darkening to cold steel. "My children called him Da."

Tammie couldn't breathe. The agony in his voice twisted her insides, but nothing could have prepared her for what he said next.

"In order to break my enchantment ... as my savior ..." His eyes locked on hers, flat, emotionless. In a flat tone, he recited the words that he'd obviously repeated many times in his mind.

By blood, by heart, by love unspoken,
The power of family now be woven.
From lone knight's path, let bonds be found,
With roots to grow in sacred ground.
Spell of ages from Master of pages.
Sacrifice fate for the knight in two cages.

"Oh my god," Tammie whispered, the ground seeming to sway beneath her. She clutched at the rough bark of the tree behind her, trying to steady herself as dizziness threatened to overwhelm her. This wasn't happening. This couldn't be happening.

Niall let out a long breath. "On the cursed day that the others and I went to meet with the Knights' Council, little did we know defending a village under attack, and crossing Meliot, sealed our fates. He punished us using his powerful magic to throw us to the other realm, where he's tortures us, sends us on useless quests and made it almost impossible to be freed. It wasn't until Tristan and Gavin were freed by your sisters that I felt a flicker of hope. Not for myself, but for the others."

Niall's voice was calm, far too calm, as though he had long since resigned himself to the cruelty of his fate. "I do not wish to father children again. Not after failing the ones I had. And even if I did ..."

"A demon holds you captive," Tammie said, watching his eyes widen. "She's real isn't she?"

"Devina. She will never release her grip on me, no matter which realm I inhabit."

His calmness cut deeper than any shouted anguish could have. He wasn't just resigned—he was utterly defeated. He'd carried this burden for centuries, and now she understood why he had never truly believed freedom was possible.

"There has to be a way," she said, her voice barely more than a whisper.

"There is not," Niall said firmly, his tone final. "I have

had a long time to consider ways I can be free. I found none. I have accepted my fate."

Niall scanned the landscape, his eyes lingering on every detail, as if committing this place to memory. She could see it now—the quiet acceptance of a man who had already decided to let go of life.

Her heart squeezed painfully in her chest. She couldn't let this happen. She wouldn't let this happen.

"Will you keep coming?" she asked, her voice edged with quiet desperation. "To help with Padraig's rescue?"

Niall turned back to her, and for a moment, something softened in his expression. "Aye. I will help Padraig."

His returning would give her time. Time to figure something out. Time to come up with a plan. One thing was certain—she wasn't leaving Niall behind, no matter what it took.

Except ... having a child. That was a line she hadn't signed up to cross with a man she barely knew.

Chapter Ten

Patrolling, and protecting the people of Atlandia alongside the princesses' warriors made time pass effortlessly. Niall didn't mind the routine, however, he missed the simpler life back at the keep. Here, he was forced to interact with others during sword practice, meals, and patrols. Often the shifters and warriors commented on his supernatural healing abilities, wanting to know how he'd acquired it.

Not wanting to speak of Meliot's curse and subsequent gift from a powerful enchantress, his brief explanation of being born with the ability seemed to satisfy whoever asked.

On that day, things looked to be a repeat of the day before and the one before that as they finished the morning meal.

"When are we returning to the other realm?" Padriag asked as they made their way to the stables.

Niall shrugged. "It is up to you."

On the opposite side, Liam huffed. "No, it is up to you

Niall. It is your time. You must release the idea that you will not be freed, because it will happen sooner than you expect."

Coming to an abrupt stop, Niall turned to Liam. With the gift of foresight, he'd learned long ago it was best to believe Liam's visions because they always came to be.

"What do you mean? How will this happen?" He grabbed Liam by the shoulders and shook him. "I do not wish to be freed, not by the terms set."

Liam shoved him away. "You know very well I have no control over what I see." The Englishman glared at him. "It is time you stop being a martyr and accept your role in this, in freeing yourself and Padriag."

It was best to remain silent. Whether his friends knew the terms of his enchantment or not, he wasn't sure. He'd shared with Tristan, and he'd probably told the others. To their credit, they'd never pushed him about it until lately. He understood, if the roles were reversed he'd do the same.

ONCE THEY ARRIVED near the border of Meliot's dark lands, where a relentless icy sleet fell from a gray sky, the men pulled their fur cloaks tighter around their shoulders and donned thick gloves to stave off the biting cold. The landscape was bleak, a desolate stretch of frozen ground and skeletal trees shrouded in mist. Just as the warriors were about to disperse into patrol groups, the thunderous pounding of hooves shattered the brittle silence, signaling a sudden shift in plans.

A single Atlandian guard galloped toward them, his steed kicking up a swirling cloud of snow and ice. He reined in abruptly, his breath coming in white puffs, urgency written across his frostbitten face. "I spotted a group of Meliot's guards headed toward the border near the village. There are only six men left to defend. Hurry!"

Without hesitation, they followed, taking the southern route, mindful of avoiding crossing the border. The cold sleet stung Niall's face, and the wind picked up, howling through the trees like a vengeful spirit. Niall could barely see his comrades, their forms mere shadows in the swirling whiteout. He whistled softly for Liam and Padraig, relieved when both answered in kind.

At last, the edge of the small village emerged through the haze. The roads between the buildings were eerily empty, the villagers undoubtedly huddled around their hearths, seeking warmth and safety from the merciless cold. The men advanced cautiously, surrounding the village and forming a tight perimeter, their figures hidden behind the skeletal tree line.

The sound of rustling leaves and the faint nickering of horses alerted them to approaching movement. Niall strained his eyes and caught the vague outline of a mounted figure in the dim light. Sword at the ready, he waited, tense and poised for action, watching the senior guard for the signal to strike.

The leader, Argo, a battle-hardened veteran, wisely held his men back until more of Meliot's forces came into view. Then, with a piercing battle cry, he led the charge, his weapon gleaming as they surged forward, weapons raised high, toward the startled enemy.

Niall's warhorse, responded instantly, muscles rippling as he charged into the fray, hooves pounding the frozen earth.

Niall guided him with practiced ease, one hand on the reins and the other gripping his sword tightly. Out of the swirling gloom, a hulking warrior in dark armor and chainmail appeared, his lance aimed squarely at Niall's heart.

With a swift swing of his sword, Niall deflected the lance, the clash of steel ringing sharply in the frigid air. The force of the blow reverberated through his arm, nearly unseating him. He grimaced at the sharp ache but maintained his grip, his gaze locked on the enemy as they passed perilously close, close enough for Niall to catch the wild gleam of fury in the man's eyes.

His horse slowed momentarily, snorting clouds of steam from his nostrils, eager to re-engage. Niall pulled the reins, wheeling the massive beast around just as his opponent did the same. Both warriors readied themselves, the dark knight leveling his lance once more, his shield poised for the next charge.

As if by mutual agreement, they spurred their mounts forward, galloping headlong toward each other. The dark warrior shouted an oath, gripping his lance with grim determination. This time, he was intent on finishing what he had started. Niall leaned low, avoiding the lethal tip of the lance to his midsection by mere inches, though it grazed his shoulder, tearing through flesh and sending a hot, searing pain down his arm. He retaliated with a swift swing of his sword, aiming for the warrior's head, but the blow was thwarted by the enemy's shield. Laughter, cruel and mocking, echoed in his ears as they parted once again. The dark warrior seemed to find a new target, because he charged away.

Irritated at not downing his opponent, Niall urged his

steed forward, weaving through the chaos of clashing swords and fallen bodies. His attention flicked to a shadowed movement at the edge of his vision. Instinctively, he ducked as an iron-spiked claymore swung toward him, narrowly missing his head. In a fluid motion, he retaliated, his sword slicing cleanly through the attacker's neck. The head hit the ground with a dull thud, followed by the lifeless body toppling moments later.

Before he could catch his breath, the dark knight charged once more, his lance poised to end Niall's life. Niall's instincts screamed a warning. He slid sideways on his saddle just in time, narrowly evading the deadly weapon. The horses collided violently, sending both riders crashing to the ground.

Dazed and bleeding, Niall struggled to breathe, the air knocked from his lungs. His shoulder throbbed, and the loss of blood was sapping his strength. He dropped to one knee, trying to gather his wits. His sword lay several feet away, lost in the impact. His opponent, seeing his vulnerability, dismounted and approached, broadsword raised high, ready to deliver the final blow.

A strange calm settled over Niall. Time seemed to slow. Death loomed near, but four centuries of battle-hardened instincts refused to surrender. Summoning the last reserves of his strength, he rolled toward a discarded claymore just as the enemy's broadsword sliced through the air where he had been.

The dark knight roared in frustration, his victory denied once again. Before he could react, Niall's horse reared up, massive hooves pawing the air above the enemy's head.

Seizing the man's momentary distraction, Niall grasped his sword and stood, ready to face his adversary.

The dark warrior turned with a snarl, charging at Niall. Their weapons clashed in a furious exchange, metal ringing against metal, each strike driven by sheer will to survive. Around them, the sounds of battle faded into the background—the groans of the dying, the clash of steel, the whinnies of frightened horses.

Spotting an opening as the dark knight drew back for a heavy strike, Niall twisted his sword and drove the blade deep into his enemy's chest. The warrior staggered, eyes wide with shock and fury, before crumpling to the ground.

Not waiting to see him fall, Niall turned, sword at the ready, prepared for the next attack. But there was none. The battle was over. Meliot's men lay dead or dying, and only a few of Atlandia's guards had fallen.

Liam and Padraig approached, their expressions a mixture of exhaustion and triumph. Ever light-hearted, Padraig raised his hand. "High five, guys. We kicked ass."

Niall shook his head, fighting the urge to smile, his heart still pounding from the fierce encounter.

Chapter Eleven

Tammie glanced between the worn book resting on her lap and the cell phone buzzing insistently on the side table, its happy ringtone jarring against the quiet of the room. Her eyes narrowed when her mother's name flashed across the screen. She held her breath, tension coiling in her chest, and exhaled in relief when the ringing stopped. No message. Her mother's silence didn't fool her—she knew it was only a temporary reprieve. The inevitable conversation loomed, thick with unanswered questions.

Since Gwen had come to Scotland, her mother had voiced that she'd prefer it if Tammie not go to Scotland. Then when Sabrina had gone, she'd actually demanded it. Why had her mother been so adamantly opposed to her traveling to Scotland? And what did that cryptic mention of her fate mean?

She couldn't run from it forever, not when the answers mattered so much. Still, facing her mother over a video call felt hollow. Tammie wanted to see her in person, to gauge her reactions, though she knew how well her mother could mask her thoughts. Frustrated with her own hesitation, she grabbed the phone, considering calling back—until voices in the hallway interrupted.

Niall's unmistakable deep timbre rumbled through the corridor. "Aye, everyone is fine. Padraig and Liam are both well."

It had been several days since she'd last seen him. Unable to resist, she rose and moved toward the library door. Niall and Tristan were walking toward the sitting room, their strides confident, purposeful. Her heart stuttered as her gaze fixed on Niall's broad shoulders, the effortless strength in his movements. Almost as if he sensed her presence, he turned, his stormy grey eyes locking with hers, intense and unreadable.

"Hello, Tamara."

The men paused, waiting for her to join them. Flanked by their imposing forms, she felt dwarfed, yet not threatened —just more aware of Niall's presence in a way that made her pulse quicken.

Once inside the sitting room, they waited for her to sit. She chose a loveseat, hoping Niall would sit beside her. He did, though he left a careful space between them, a distance she wanted to close.

Tristan poured himself a drink. "What could possibly interest Meliot in that particular border region? There's nothing there but a simple village."

Niall shook his head, and for the first time, she noticed a faint bruise along his jawline. Concern flared.

"What happened?" she asked, leaning toward him.

"We fought alongside Atlandia's warriors to defend the village from an attack." His voice was steady, but he avoided her gaze.

"Are you all right?" She reached out to touch his face, but he pulled back, evading her hand.

"I'm well."

She frowned, withdrawing her hand, irritation flickering in her chest. "Your charming personality seems to be intact, at least," she muttered.

Tristan cleared his throat. "I will leave you both to talk."

The moment he left, Niall rose and moved to the window, his back rigid, his focus on the world beyond the glass. Something in his posture made her chest tighten—distance, isolation, a quiet pain he refused to share.

"The sky is different in the other realm," he murmured, as if speaking more to himself than to her. "More purple than blue. Any day now, three moons will grace the sky and remain for several weeks. Padraig's enchantment is tied to that."

Tammie stepped closer, curiosity piqued. "How many moons are there normally?"

"Two, most nights. Sometimes three suns during the day, depending on the season."

"And yet, it's a frozen land? How does that work?"

"Only certain regions are frozen. Where we lived, the weather was much like here."

She moved to stand beside him. "How are the three moons connected to Padraig's enchantment?"

"That's for Padraig to explain, not me." He didn't turn, his voice distant. "I'd rather not get it wrong."

Frustration simmered beneath her skin. She turned to face him directly, determined. "Fine. Then let's talk about you."

"There's nothing to discuss."

Her jaw tightened. "Can't you try, for once? You mentioned something about a family. What exactly are the terms of breaking your enchantment?"

His lips pressed into a hard line, and she knew that look —he wouldn't talk. But she couldn't back down now.

"Niall, for the love of God, can't you let someone in? Let someone help you?"

He finally met her gaze, his grey eyes dark and turbulent, and for a moment she thought he might answer. Instead, he turned away. "I must take my leave."

An idea struck. Before he could disappear, she grabbed his shirt, forcing him to stop.

"Were there three moons when you first fell under the enchantment?"

His brows lifted in surprise at her sudden shift. "Aye, there were."

"Then maybe the approaching three moons are tied to the attack on that village."

He stilled, considering her words. "You may be right."

Emboldened, she pressed on. "Could Meliot be after the women from that village?"

"Aye." His tone grew more serious. "That could be his goal."

Their eyes locked, tension thick between them. She wanted to shout, to beg him to open up, to tell her what she needed to know before it was too late.

"Please, Niall," she whispered, her voice trembling with urgency. "Tell me what it takes to break your curse. Tell me how to save you. Do you know more than the words you spoke when we were last together?"

His gaze darkened, but no answer came. Instead, he closed the distance between them, his lips capturing hers in a kiss that stole her breath. The tenderness caught her off guard, yet she leaned into it, surrendering to the soft, insistent pressure of his mouth. His arms encircled her, pulling her close, and she let herself fall into him, hoping to convey what her words could not.

Choose life, Niall. Don't give up.

Her hands slid over the hard planes of his arms, fingers threading through his thick hair as he deepened the kiss. When he drew her against him, the warmth of his body sent shivers racing through her. His lips moved to her throat, and she arched into him, her knees weakening under the sweet torment of his touch.

"Niall..." she whispered, urging him on.

He silenced her with another kiss, deeper this time, more desperate. Just as she thought she might break from wanting him, he released her abruptly, stepping back. His storm-dark eyes met hers, both of them gasping for breath.

Tammie reached for him, unwilling to let him go. "Stay, Niall. Don't leave."

But before she could say more, he vanished.

"Damn it," she hissed, her hands clenching in the empty air where he'd stood.

Three lives rescued
Three moons high
Two hearts restored
One must die

PADRIAG'S SPELL WAS OMINOUS. He'd repeated several times, then Tammie and her sisters had dissected every word for hours.

Too tired to remain seated, Tammie stalked from one side of the library to the other. Gwen and Tristan sat on a couch and watched her. She'd repeated the verses so many times; she could say them in her sleep.

"Niall said the three moons would rise in a few days." She stopped pacing and looked to her sister's husband. "What is the significance of it?"

Tristan shrugged a broad shoulder. "It's a rare occurrence in the alter-world, happens every hundred years or so. I don't recall there being anything different during the last time it happened." He gave her a worry-filled look. "We think that perhaps it means that the last knights will be able to break free of the enchantment, but someone will die."

"Oh, I hope not," Gwen cried. "That would be horrible. After all that time in captivity, only to die upon being rescued."

Liam materialized. The knight was so bundled in furs, only his blue eyes were visible. He began to immediately remove the layers, dropping them on the floor.

When only a tunic and breeches remained he finally

addressed them. "The icing began when I left. I didn't want to chance returning in the midst of it without being properly dressed." He explained.

Tristan stood and went to him, placing his hand on the Brit's shoulder. "Liam, how are you?"

"Well, but more than ready for all of this to be over." Liam told them. "We have volunteered to remain behind at Middlesex to defend the village from further attacks from Meliot. It is not the best of circumstances, but at least it gives us the freedom to return here at will."

Gwen stood and went toward the doorway. "I will get you something to eat. Please sit down Liam, I'll be right back."

He followed Tristan to the desk and sat. Tammie studied Liam. With the whitest blonde hair she'd ever seen, clear complexion, and ice-blue eyes, he was very handsome. She knew he could leave the alter-world at will. His enchantment was broken. Yet, she wondered why he chose to remain behind until the other two left. He was in love with a man named John, and yet, didn't seem in a hurry to remain with his lover. Was it loyalty?

As if sensing her though process, his gaze met hers. "I am very anxious to see John again, but we've decided it's best for him to remain in Edinburgh for now. It would be too tempting for him to utter the words that would force me to break my word to remain in the other region.

"Of course," Tammie told him, warmth filling her. "I am just in awe of your loyalty and the strong ties you men share."

He smiled at her and nodded. "It is rare indeed to form

such a strong bond with others. Yet in our circumstances, it was not our choice."

"Oh I think it was," Tammie insisted. "You could be in Edinburgh and away from all this; you choose to remain so that you can be of help."

Tristan patted Liam's shoulder. "Tammie is correct. Do not take away from what you are doing for us."

"Liam," Tammie started. "Do you have any idea regarding the conditions of Niall's enchantment? You have the ability to see the future. Have you at any time seen anything that could help?"

He shook his head. "Niall has never spoken of the terms. None of us ever pushed him, knowing it must be a rather difficult thing for him. I know he rarely sleeps well. Of all of us, he is the one found pacing the keep at night while the rest of us slept. I sometimes wondered if breaking his enchantment had something to do with whatever happens to him while he sleeps."

"I think he is attacked at night. I am not sure how often." Tammie met each of their gazes. "I believe he thinks that it will continue even if he breaks free and comes here. Is that possible?"

"I do not know," Liam replied. "But it's possible."

"I will have to confront that woman, thing, whatever she is. He is going to tell me everything." Tammie frowned at the thought.

Both men had identical reactions, their lips pressed together to keep from saying anything.

Tammie waved her hand at them. "I know he will probably react badly, but we're running out of time. I am going to have to go at him with everything I've got. There has to be some way of getting him to talk."

"PROMISE me you'll come home immediately." Her mother's voice, edged with urgency and something close to desperation, echoed through the phone. "You must listen to me. You can't stay in Scotland any longer. It's too dangerous."

Tammie inhaled deeply, willing herself to remain calm, though frustration prickled beneath her skin. "If you'd just explain what this supposed danger is, I might consider it. But you can't expect me to drop everything and board a plane without a reason."

"Tamara ..." Her mother's voice hardened, using her full name as she always did when anger flared. "I need you to trust me. It's not safe for you there, and I'll explain everything when you get home."

"I'm sorry, Mom. I will call you later. Call me if you want to tell me why you're so against me being here. I love you." Tammie's tone was firm as she ended the call before her mother continued.

Anticipating that her mother would call back immediately, she powered off her phone and stuffed it into her pocket. Her heart raced, more from the tension in her mother's voice than from her own irritation.

The house was eerily silent as she wandered through it. The library was empty, as was the sitting room. Even the kitchen, where the scent of baking or simmering soup usually lingered, was void of life. She glanced toward the stairs and hesitated, debating whether to check upstairs. Gwen had mentioned staying close by since they expected tension to rise with the impending third moon in the alter-world.

Climbing to the second floor, she found the master bedroom door slightly ajar. Peeking inside, she was surprised to find it empty. A pang of unease rippled through her. If Gwen and Tristan had gone somewhere, they would have told her, especially now, when every movement felt crucial.

Crossing quickly to the window, Tammie scanned the garden below. No sign of Gwen or Tristan. Her eyes landed on the housekeeper, bustling across the yard with a bundle of linens in her arms.

Tammie raced from the room and down the stairs. She dashed outside, cutting across the lawn to intercept the housekeeper.

"Have you seen my sister or Lord McRainey?"

"They're at the stables checking on the horses since Mr. Campbell is away," the housekeeper replied without slowing her pace. "Your sister said she'd be back soon to discuss dinner plans."

Tammie offered a distracted nod and returned to her bedroom. As she reached the hallway, a sudden chill washed over her. She paused, instinctively glancing behind her, and gasped. A figure loomed in the shadows, cloaked in thick furs. Before she could scream, his hand clamped over her mouth.

"It's me, Niall."

Relief coursed through her, and she relaxed, allowing him to lower his hand. "You really need to stop appearing out of nowhere," she muttered, leading him into her room. "I was just about to grab my spell book. I found something interesting—something that might help with your enchantment."

Niall shrugged off his furs, and Tammie hesitated midstride. It was impossible to look away. He filled out the dark jeans and fitted sweater far too well, his broad shoulders and lean hips making her pulse flutter involuntarily.

"Er ... anyway," she stammered, turning quickly to rummage through her things. She snatched the spell book from her bed, only to back straight into Niall's solid frame.

"Where's Tristan?" His voice was low, his breath warm against her cheek. He stood so close, she could feel the heat radiating from him.

Without turning, afraid she might do something reckless, she said, "Tristan and Gwen are at the stables. Sabrina and Gavin are still at Castle Campbell. They'll be back by morning."

"I came to say goodbye."

The words hit her like a slap. She whirled around, bumping into his chest. "Goodbye? What do you mean?"

"I must stay behind if Padraig is to be freed," he said quietly, his expression unreadable.

Fury ignited in her chest. "That's it? You're giving up? Letting Meliot win without even trying to fight?" Her fists clenched, and before she could stop herself, she punched him square in the chest. Pain shot up her hand, and she winced. "Ow! Damn it."

Niall reached for her hand, but she yanked it back. "Don't you dare touch me, you stubborn, insufferable man."

"You don't understand the full nature of my enchantment," he said, his storm-grey eyes darkening with frustration.

"Oh, of course I don't," she shot back, stepping closer until they were nearly nose to nose. "You refuse to tell me everything! You won't raise a finger to help yourself, and yet you expect us to somehow figure it all out and accept it."

His jaw clenched, the muscle ticking beneath his skin. "It's impossible—"

"No! Nothing is impossible," she snapped. "If you want to sulk in the corner while we do all the work, fine. But don't you dare tell me it can't be done."

"I will help free Padraig. You should focus your efforts on him, not me."

Silence hung between them, tension crackling in the air like an impending storm. Slowly, Niall reached out, his fingers brushing along her jawline. His touch was unexpectedly gentle, his eyes softening. "You're a brave woman, Tamara. My crusader."

Before she could respond, his mouth descended to hers, fierce and demanding. She met him with equal intensity, threading her fingers through his hair as he pulled her tightly against him. There was nothing gentle about the way he kissed her—this was raw, wild need.

With a growl, Niall swept her up, and they tumbled onto the bed. His hands moved urgently, pulling at her clothes as she did the same.

Finally skin met skin, heat rising between them like a flame that refused to be doused. Tammie arched into him, reveling in the feel of his hard body, the strength that surrounded her.

"Niall ..." she whispered, her voice a breathless plea as he plunged into her, his movements slow and steady, each thrust drawing her closer to the edge.

Their rhythm quickened, and Tamara met every single one of his drives, arching up, their bodies colliding until the intensity was such that they were both panting, their blood on fire, unable to stop as they chased the elusive release that seemed just out of reach. Tammie dug her fingernails into the small of his back, somehow needing him closer, deeper.

His heavy breaths fanned across her face as their eyes locked. He was so breathtakingly handsome, and even in the throes of passion, the storm in his gray eyes remained.

When he threw back his head, the thick cords of his neck and shoulders bulged. Tammie began to lose control, her breathing hitching until her body and mind exploded, flying, tumbling, reeling.

Her hoarse cry intermixed with Niall's deep groan as he too fell over the cliff, his huge body shuddering before collapsing.

For a moment, neither moved, their breaths mingling in the stillness.

"Stay with me," she whispered, her arms wrapping around him as if to keep him from vanishing again.

"I will ... for a while," he murmured, pressing a soft kiss to her hair.

They lay entwined, the weight of unspoken words between them. Tammie traced lazy circles on his back, savoring the rare moment of peace. But even in this quiet, she knew the stillness wouldn't last.

The fight wasn't over—not yet.

Tammie ran her hands over his back, massaging the hard planes. She smiled when he sighed at her touch.

"I should move. I am crushing you," Niall told her and tried to move.

She wrapped her arms around him and held him in place. "Not yet." When she nuzzled his neck, he relaxed again.

"I will stay with you for a bit," he told her lifting his head and looking at her. Then he leaned forward and kissed her. This kiss was soft, the kiss of a well-satisfied man.

Reluctantly, she allowed him to roll off of her, and she snuggled against his side. He remained silent, his fingers tracing small circles on her arm.

"What are you thinking?" Tammie asked him and pressed a kiss to his jaw.

"I can't remember ever feeling like this," Niall replied surprising her with his candor. "I could remain here in this room, with you in bed forever."

"We would eventually have to find food," Tammie teased nibbling at his ear.

His low growl told that he enjoyed the sensations. "Aye, we would."

She raised and leaned on his chest. With a finger, she outlined his lips. "I suppose if it came to life or death by hunger, we could just call and ask the housekeeper to bring food and eat in bed."

Niall nodded. His lips curved. Her breath caught. It was the first time she'd seen him smile.

The smile vanished as if he caught himself. And she kissed his lips. "Tell me about Atlandia."

He put his arm behind his head. "It's ugly."

Tammie laughed. "Wow, that draws a great picture."

"I suppose it could also be described as beautiful, white as far as the eye can see. Unlike the area where we lived, which resembles this realm, Atlandia is stark. Everything is covered in snow and ice. There are some trees that barely survive, but for the most part, you can travel for days and not see another living creature."

"Yet some people continue to live there."

"Aye, for the most part in small villages that are supported by the Royals. The village of Middlesex is protected on one side by a mountain, so the air is not as frigid. They manage to grow some crops and raise wooly animals, much like cows, but smaller."

"What a hard life," Tammie replied, then lay her head on his chest. "I don't think I want to visit."

He didn't respond and she wondered if he'd fallen asleep until he kissed the top of her head.

Tammie took a deep breath. "I want to ask you a question. Promise you won't be angry, just answer my question."

At his lack of response, she looked up at him. "Promise."

With a slight nod, his wary eyes met hers. "All right."

"Is part of your enchantment something that happens in your dreams or in your sleep?"

Niall didn't need to reply. She knew she'd guessed right at the stiffening of his jaw and the way his brows drew together before he caught himself and erased all expression from his face. "No."

"One night, while I slept, it was as if I slipped into your dream," Tammie told him without inflection in her voice.

"Dreams are different than dream travel," he told her in a flat voice. "Not everything is easily defined."

Once again, Tammie ensured to keep her tone neutral. "I dreamed about you, that you were being tortured, that this dark-haired woman threatened you."

Niall went to move away, but she pretended not to notice and lay her head on his chest. "I suppose I had this dream because I constantly worry. But it was so vivid. In my dream, I was powerful, and I was able to keep the woman from hurting you. Isn't that interesting?"

"It is," Niall replied, his entire body still.

"Not exactly pillow talk, is it," Tammie teased. "I would rather do something else than to talk about such dreary things."

She ran her hand down his thigh, at the same time she flicked her tongue out at his nipple, loving it when his breath caught.

Slowly, sliding her fingers up his inner thigh, she took his sex in hand, curving her fingers around the hardening member. Niall closed his eyes.

Trailing kisses down his chest, she slid her hand up and down on his shaft, delighted when he bucked into her hold.

She had part of the answer, on how to fight his enchantment. In the other realm, she was powerful. Somehow, she'd find a way to go there. Once there, she'd confront the dark-haired demon.

Her lips curved as she took Niall's shaft into her mouth, relishing his grunts of pleasure.

Chapter Twelve

Niall jolted awake, heart pounding, disoriented for a moment before the weight of reality settled over him. He'd meant to stay vigilant, to fight the ever-encroaching pull of sleep, but his exhaustion had won. Yet, for the first time in what felt like an eternity, he didn't regret it. His body felt lighter, rested in a way he hadn't been in months. The soft warmth beside him stirred something deep within, a fleeting sense of peace.

He closed his eyes briefly, savoring the quiet intimacy of the moment, the scent of her hair lingering in the air. Tamara.

His gaze drifted down to her face, serene in sleep, golden strands of hair framing her delicate features. Her lashes fanned against her skin, and her lips, slightly parted, tempted him anew. She was more than beautiful; she was life, fire, passion. Memories of their night together flickered through his mind, and heat stirred in his veins, as vivid as the sunlight filtering in through the window.

But the light brought more than warmth—it brought reality. The morning rays scattered across the chamber, bright and unyielding, as if mocking the fragile reprieve of the night before. Niall sat up sharply, a sudden awareness creeping over him. He had lingered in this realm longer than ever before. The pull that should have dragged him back to the other world was conspicuously absent. Strange. He flexed his fingers, testing for any sign of the enchantment tightening its grip on him. Nothing. Was it possible? Could he truly have found a place where Devina's reach didn't extend?

Still, he could not ignore the warning prickle sliding down his spine. Something was off. He scanned the room, his senses on high alert, but nothing seemed out of place. Only the soft rustle of Tamara shifting in her sleep broke the silence. Even in this quiet moment, she sought him unconsciously, curling into the space he had left behind, a faint smile curving her lips.

He moved with deliberate care, sliding from the bed so as not to wake her. His eyes lingered on her sleeping form, committing every detail to memory—her golden hair tangled across the pillow, the peaceful expression that softened her features. How had she slipped past his defenses so completely? He shouldn't have let her in. He couldn't afford to.

There was still too much to do, and he couldn't allow himself the luxury of hope. Last night, he had been close to surrendering to that daring temptation—hope. With Tamara in his arms, the possibility of freedom had felt almost tangible, as though her touch could dissolve the darkness that clung to him like a second skin. But he knew better. He couldn't risk it. He couldn't risk *her*.

A sudden tug, sharp and relentless, pulled at his very being. Time was up. He had to go. Quickly, he dressed, sliding on jeans, shirt, sock and shoes. Next, he fastened the belts of daggers across his body with practiced efficiency. Lastly he grabbed the thick cloak that had been strewn across a chair. The fur felt heavy in his hand as he hesitated by the bed. This had to be the last time. For her sake. Returning would only give her false hope. He would never father another child, not after failing the ones with his first wife.

Besides, he would not—*could not*—ever risk bringing a child into this cursed life.

Tamara let out a soft murmur, shifting slightly, her hair gleaming like spun gold in the morning light. His heart twisted painfully. How was it that she had come to mean so much in so little time? He'd cared deeply for his late wife, but never before had he felt so linked to someone's very existence. Tamara had found her way into his heart, an anchor he hadn't realized he needed until it was too late.

He reached out, fingers hovering inches from her cheek, craving one final touch, one final memory to hold. But he stopped himself. If he touched her now, he wouldn't be able to leave.

He shouldn't have allowed things to go this far. Shouldn't have let her break through the walls he had carefully built around himself. She would hurt when he didn't return, and he hated himself for it. Yet what choice did he have? The curse was his burden alone to bear and dragging her into his torment would be the cruelest betrayal of all.

Steeling himself, he stepped back, eyes never leaving her face. He would carry this moment with him, relive the memories of her touch, her smile, her laughter, until his final breath. It was all he could allow himself. A life of darkness awaited him, but for these few fleeting hours, he had known light. And it was enough to carry him through what lay ahead.

Without another glance, he turned toward the door, the ache in his chest a heavy reminder of what he could never truly have.

The pull to return to the other realm gripped Niall with increasing urgency. He paused, centering himself, unsure exactly where he was being drawn. He prayed silently that upon his return, all would be well—that Padraig and Liam were unharmed. Bracing himself, he gave in to the relentless tug, and in an instant, Tamara's bedchamber dissolved around him.

He reappeared in the familiar camp near Middlesex, the cold air biting at his skin. The scent of damp earth and burning wood filled his lungs, a stark contrast to the warmth he had just left behind. The village lay in uneasy quiet, shadows stretching long under the pale morning light. They had been fighting Meliot's forces for days, and the tension in the air felt as thick as the frost coating the ground.

Niall pulled his cloak tighter around him, shielding himself from the bitter chill as he made his way toward the promise of warmth inside a makeshift tent. The heavy fabric rustled behind him as he entered, and he was immediately greeted by Padraig's grim expression.

"You were gone a long time," Padraig said, his voice edged with both relief and frustration. "I was worried."

Niall met his friend's gaze, guilt flickering briefly in his eyes. "I fell asleep. I don't know how I managed to stay there for so long without being pulled back. I'm sorry for causing you concern."

Padraig studied him for a moment, his sharp eyes taking in every detail. "You look rested. That's good." Without further comment, he led Niall toward a round metal furnace in the center of the tent where a fire blazed, casting flickering shadows and radiating much-needed heat.

Something about Padraig seemed off, a tension in his posture, a heaviness in his tone. Niall waited until they were far enough from prying ears before speaking. "What's wrong? You're holding something back." He glanced around the dim interior. "Where's Liam?"

Padraig's jaw tightened before he answered, his voice flat. "He went to see John. Said he'd return soon."

Crossing the tent, Padraig sank heavily onto his bed, his shoulders slumped in a way that made Niall uneasy. "I have no enchantress," he muttered, his voice laced with quiet despair. "Soon, the three moons will be at their highest."

Over the years, Niall had seen Padraig endure moments of frustration and discouragement, but this was different. The despondency in his friend was palpable, weighing down the air between them.

"There's still time," Niall said gently, though he felt the weight of his own doubts pressing against his chest. "The moons won't be at their peak for another sennight. Don't give up yet."

Padraig's gaze met his, and the raw desperation there made Niall's breath hitch. "I'm tired, Niall. I understand now—why you stopped hoping, why you don't try to break free anymore. Maybe ... maybe it's not meant to be. For either of us." His voice dropped lower, trembling with exhaustion. "Lately, all I want to do is lie down and sleep for days. To stop fighting, stop trying ... just stop."

Hearing Padraig voice what had long haunted his own thoughts unsettled Niall more than he cared to admit. For years, he had carried the weight of his hopelessness in silence. Now, hearing it reflected in his friend's words felt like staring into a mirror he wished to shatter.

Padraig leaned forward, resting his elbows on his knees, his head bowed. "Maybe we should leave. Go back to the keep. I don't want to do this anymore. I'm so damn tired."

Niall's instinct was to reassure him, to insist that hope still existed, but no words came. What could he say? Too much needed to happen—each step an impossible challenge. Both their fates hinged on a chain of events so unlikely it was a cruel joke. He couldn't deny it. Padraig wasn't wrong.

With a heavy sigh, Niall rubbed a hand over his face, the faint scent of Tamara's skin still lingering on his fingers. How foolish he had been, allowing himself a taste of hope the night before. A fool's luxury. Now, faced with Padraig's despair, hope felt even further out of reach.

He turned to his friend who sat unmoving, staring at the ground as though searching for answers in the dirt beneath his boots. "Let's wait for Liam," Niall said quietly. "We'll hear what he has to say. If, by morning, you still want to return to the keep ... I'll go with you."

Padraig didn't respond, but the slump of his shoulders deepened, as though the weight of the world had pressed harder against him. Niall could offer no promises, no grand speeches of hope. All he could do was stand by his friend and face whatever came next—together.

IT WAS late in the evening when Liam arrived, just as Niall and Padriag prepared for bed. The Englishman walked toward them, elegant, even covered in thick furs. He went to his cot and removed the cloak, hanging it carefully on a rope they'd strung from one corner to the other in order to hang wet clothes and allow the garments to dry.

Liam's icy blue gaze went from Niall to Padriag. "The answer is no. Whatever you two miserable idiots are planning, it will not come to pass."

With a huff, Padriag shook his head. "Niall and I have discussed it. Breaking our curses is an impossibility we must all accept."

Raking a hand down his face, Liam blew out a frustrated breath. "If that were true, would I keep returning here?" He held up a hand. "Do not answer that. Because we all know the answer. "I would not. I have seen it, not the how, but the result of all of this," he motioned around the enclosure. "In the end all will be well."

"There are many ways things could be well," Padriag replied. "Do you see either of us over there? In the other realm?"

Liam's mouth opened, but he didn't speak. This was all the fuel Padriag needed. "You don't. I, too, sense that the final chapter of this story is coming to an end. Even if not a happy ending, it will be an ending. A satisfactory one."

BEFORE SHE OPENED HER EYES, Tammie was sharply aware of two unsettling truths—Niall was gone, and something was wrong. Deeply wrong. The room wavered, a peculiar, disorienting motion that jolted her fully awake. Her heart pounded as she sat up, scanning the empty room, though the silence carried an eerie weight, as if something unseen lingered in the shadows.

Before she could gather her thoughts, the entire room tilted abruptly to one side, and she barely stifled a scream, gripping the cold iron bars of the headboard with trembling hands. A dream. It had to be a dream. Somehow, she needed to wake up.

The room swayed again, more violently this time, and her stomach rebelled, nausea rising fast. Desperate for the solid comfort of the floor beneath her feet, Tammie slid off the bed but immediately collapsed as the shifting ground threw her off balance.

"Help!" she screamed, her voice echoing strangely. "Someone help me!" The walls didn't just reflect her cry— they seemed to absorb it, muffling the sound.

The biting wind that rushed through the suddenly open window made her gasp, whipping the thin curtains sideways in a chaotic dance. Struggling to her feet, she tried to keep her balance, only to fall again onto all fours.

Then, a figure loomed in the window—a man, tall and

draped in heavy furs like those Niall had worn the previous night. His broad shoulders filled the narrow frame, and his dark eyes, nearly black, glinted beneath the edge of a fur-lined hood. His face remained partially obscured, save for those piercing eyes, the darkest Tammie had ever seen.

"I've come for you on behalf of Meliot." The man's deep voice was accented and harsh, perhaps German, though she couldn't be sure.

He stepped fully into the room, pulling back his hood to reveal a ruggedly handsome face marred by deep claw marks that scored one cheek. His gaze swept over her with unnerving intensity. Instinctively, Tammie grabbed a blanket from the bed and clutched it to her chest, shielding her bare skin. "Get out of my room!" she demanded, her voice trembling between fear and fury.

"You must dress," he said, his tone steady, unyielding.

Tammie let out a frustrated scream, her fury only growing when no one responded. "I would if you'd stop making the room move! I'm going to be sick!" she snapped, glaring up at him. "Who are you?"

For a moment, he stilled, as if her defiance caught him off guard. "Who I am does not matter," he finally replied.

The swaying ceased, as suddenly as it had started. Grateful for the reprieve, Tammie took several deep breaths, willing her roiling stomach to settle. Without taking her eyes off the stranger, she snatched up her jeans and a T-shirt, pulling them on with quick, jerky movements. As she reached for her socks and shoes, she glanced toward the door, weighing her chances of escape.

"I'm not going anywhere with you," she said, forcing

defiance into her voice as she slipped on her shoes and grabbed her jacket from the back of a chair. She hoped he couldn't hear the rapid pounding of her heart. "Where are you taking me?"

He said nothing, watching her with quiet intensity as she dressed. His gaze never wavered, following her every movement like a hawk tracking prey.

Thinking fast, Tammie decided on a distraction. Hands on her hips, she fixed him with what she hoped was a skeptical glare. "I bet you're not from this world."

"We must go," he repeated, his tone colder now.

"I don't think so," she said, lifting her chin. "I have to relieve myself."

The man blinked, clearly taken aback. "What?"

"I have to use the bathroom," Tammie said, pointing toward the small door. "Unless you want me to pee everywhere while you're kidnapping me."

He hesitated, then moved to the bathroom door, peering inside as though expecting an ambush.

The perfect opening. Tammie bolted for the main door, fingers brushing the doorknob before a powerful arm wrapped around her waist, pinning her against him. She kicked and thrashed, but his grip didn't loosen. "Let go of me!" she yelled, twisting and turning, but he held her easily, his strength far beyond anything she could match.

"If you must relieve yourself, do so now," he said, his voice edged with reluctant patience.

He released her, and Tammie stumbled toward the bathroom, slamming the door shut behind her. Her hands shook as she fumbled with the lock. After using the toilet, she splashed cold water on her face, forcing herself to think. Whoever he was, wherever he planned to take her, it couldn't be anywhere good.

An idea struck her. Grabbing the toothpaste, she quickly squeezed out a message on the mirror with her finger. *Help. Taken to other realm. Meliot.*

Just as she finished, the door opened.

Tammie stepped out of the bathroom, careful to keep her expression neutral. She prayed the stranger wouldn't notice the hastily written message on the mirror behind her. He stood waiting, his dark eyes locked on her, unblinking.

"We must leave," he said again, his tone firmer this time.

Tammie took a deliberate step back, feigning reluctance. "At least tell me who you are," she said, hoping to stall further. "If you expect me to go with you, I deserve to know that much."

"I am called Gunther," he replied with a slight incline of his head. His voice, deep and gravelly, carried an air of authority. "That is all you need to know for now."

Gunther. Definitely German, she thought, filing the information away. Though it gave her no clearer picture of what she was dealing with, at least it was something.

"Where you're taking me?" Tammie asked again, her hands clenched into fists at her sides. "And why?"

Gunther didn't reply. Instead, he grabbed her arm and pulled her toward the window. Tammie struggled, but his grip was unbreakable.

"Wait! Wait!" she cried, panic flaring. "We can't go out the window! We are on the second floor."

Gunther didn't seem to hear her. In one swift motion, he

wrapped his arms around her and before she could scream, he stepped onto the window ledge and leaped into a swirly void.

The wind roared around them as they fell, the world a blur of dark sky and streaking light. Tammie clung to Gunther, her heart hammering wildly, her already weak stomach threatening. She squeezed her eyes shut taking shallow breaths, praying not to get sick.

They landed hard on a blanket of snow, Gunther absorbing the brunt of the impact as they tumbled across the frozen ground. The surroundings were barren, ice- and snow-covered landscape as far as she could see. It was like what she imagined the Arctic was like.

Gunther rose smoothly, as if the fall had been nothing more than a mild inconvenience. He scanned their surroundings, sword in hand. Tammie followed his gaze, shivering violently.

She scrambled away from him and began to throw up. Just when she thought it stopped, her stomach would lurch again. Blindly, she stumbled to what looked to be a frozen tree and leaned on it, willing her stomach to still.

The cold was unlike anything she had ever felt, sharp and biting, sinking into her bones as if her clothing was inconsequential. Shivering so hard, her teeth chattering, it was astounding her they didn't shatter into pieces.

"Where are we?" she asked, her voice trembling.

Gunther didn't answer. He motioned her closer. "We must share the cloak to avert the cold."

Tammie backed away from him. "Stay away from me. I would rather freeze then get close to you."

"You will freeze without this," He told her, his eyes flat. Removing the cloak from around his shoulders, he tossed it at her. "Put it on and follow me. We have to go." He turned and walked away.

The relief from the cold was immediate. The warmth of the fur and his body seeped into her. Tammie held the cloak tight, picking it up from the ground so she could walk and not trip. She considered going in the opposite direction, but besides the fact that he'd probably catch her, she didn't want to die of exposure.

No other practical choice, she followed after him.

They trudged through the snow in silence, the only sounds their labored breathing and the crunch of ice beneath their boots. The wind howled around them, carrying with it strange, haunting echoes that set Tammie's nerves on edge.

A sudden growl broke the silence.

Tammie whirled around, heart in her throat. Four massive wolves, their fur a mix of gray and white, stood at the edge of a nearby ridge. Their eyes glowed an unnatural yellow, and their fangs gleamed in the dim light.

"Oh my god," she whispered. "This cannot be happening."

Gunther didn't hesitate. He drew his sword with a swift, practiced motion and stepped in front of her. "Stay close," he ordered. "If they attack, we will run."

Easier said than done, Tammie thought, but she nodded, too terrified to argue.

The wolves advanced slowly, their movements predatory and precise. Gunther tightened his grip on his sword, readying himself for a fight. The inevitable happened and

Tammie tripped on the cloak falling hard onto the frozen ground.

In the next moment, Gunther picked her up, threw her over his shoulder, and took off at a hard run. The wolves gave chase, their huge fangs exposed, growls seeming to bounce off the trees. She'd never seen wolves in real life, but even to her untrained eye, she knew these massive animals were not normal.

Upon reaching the edge of the woods, the wolves stopped and let out long howls. Gunther put her down, his chest heaving from the exertion of the run, but still he pulled her forward, trekking at a quick pace.

They reached a gloomy castle with turrets that jutted into the foggy dark purple skies. This was definitely not a fairytale structure, more something from nightmares.

Tammie's legs were trembling so badly she could barely stand. Enormous iron gates loomed before them, flanked by black wolves almost as large as the ones that had chased them. Unlike the others, these wolves didn't move. They stood perfectly still, like statues, their glowing eyes fixed on her.

Gunther pushed open the gates, the heavy iron creaking loudly in the stillness. They entered a courtyard shrouded in mist, the ground beneath their feet slick with ice. Tammie hesitated, her instincts screaming at her to turn back, to run. She peered over her shoulder at the expanse of ice-covered land and forest. A forest where huge wolves who could eat her alive would undoubtedly find her. There was nowhere to go.

She quickened her steps until walking next to Gunther.

The cloak over her shoulders seemed to grow heavier as they approached the main doors of the castle.

Two hulking figures emerged from the shadows. They were larger than any man she had ever seen, their faces scarred, twisted, and beast-like, their eyes as black as the void.

"We'll take her," one of them growled, stepping forward.

Tammie couldn't breathe. Terror seized her. What was happening? This was definitely more than she'd ever expected in her quest to rescue Niall.

When the beastlike beings moved forward, Gunther pushed Tammie behind him, blocking their path. "I was instructed to deliver her personally." His tone was laced with warning.

"Your duty was to bring her here, nothing else," one of them replied. "Move aside."

Without waiting for Gunther to move, one of them seized Tammie by the arm, his grip like iron. Tammie didn't try to fight them knowing it would be useless. Any feeble attempts to get away from them could result in them killing her on the spot.

When she looked back, Gunther's gaze met hers briefly, and for a moment, she thought she saw regret in his eyes.

Tammie's heart pounded in her chest as the beastly guards dragged her down a dim corridor lined with stone walls, torches flickering weakly in iron sconces. The air was damp and cold, carrying the faint scent of mildew. Every instinct told her to fight. A sizzle bubbled under her skin.

What it was that coursed through her, she had no idea, but whatever it was, it couldn't help her. These creatures were far stronger than she was, and the odds weren't in her favor.

They stopped in front of a heavy wooden door reinforced with iron bands. One of the beasts pulled a large key from his belt, inserting it into the lock with a loud *clank*. The door groaned as it swung open, revealing a dimly lit room beyond. Without ceremony, they shoved her inside and slammed the door shut behind her.

The finality of the lock turning sent a chill down her spine.

Never in her life had she been more terrified. This was the thing of nightmares, something that should never truly exist.

Still shivering from the cold and fear, Tammie took a moment to assess her surroundings. The room was large but sparsely furnished. A massive four-poster bed draped in dark velvet dominated the space, its canopy draping down to the floor. A simple wooden washstand stood against one wall, holding a ceramic pitcher and basin. To the side, a narrow doorway led to what appeared to be a rudimentary toilet.

Despite the castle's ominous exterior, the room itself was oddly elegant, as though it had once belonged to someone of importance. Although the thick iron-reinforced door reminded her that it was still a prison.

Forcing herself to stay calm, Tammie crossed the room to the narrow window. Peering through it, she saw that this side of the castle was perched on the edge of a steep cliff. Beyond the jagged rocks below lay an endless expanse of white, the icy landscape stretching as far as the eye could see. Escape from this height was impossible.

She turned away from the window, biting her lip as she tried to think. *Think, Tammie. There's got to be a way out of this.*

Her thoughts were interrupted by a faint tapping sound.

Tap. Tap. Tap.

Tammie frowned, listening intently. The sound came again, steady and deliberate. She moved toward the wall, pressing her ear against the cold stone.

"Can you hear me?" a muffled female voice called out.

"Yes!" Tammie answered, relief flooding through her. "Who are you? Can you help me get out of here?"

"I'm Erin. Erin McGuire," the voice replied. "I can't help you. I'm locked in too."

"How long have you been here?" Tammie asked, her voice lowering to a whisper, though she wasn't sure why.

"This is my second day. They haven't hurt me," Erin replied. "Someone brought me food once, but that's it. I have no idea why I'm here."

Tammie leaned closer to the wall, feeling a little comforted by the presence of another person, even if she couldn't see her. "I'm Tammie Lockhart. Do you know anything about what's going on? Who's behind this?"

"No," Erin replied, her voice tinged with fear. "But I heard the guards talking about someone named Meliot. Does that mean anything to you?"

Tammie's blood ran cold. Despite her suspicions that the evil, powerful wizard was involved, hearing it made her stomach sink with dread.

Before she could say more, the sound of heavy footsteps

echoed from the hallway outside her door. Tammie backed away from the wall, heart racing.

"They're coming," she whispered. "Stay quiet."

"Tap twice if you're okay," Erin said quickly.

Tammie tapped twice on the wall, and Erin responded in kind. Just as she moved away, the door creaked open, and a hulking figure stepped into the room. It wasn't Gunther this time, but another guard, his face half-hidden beneath a hood. He carried a tray of food, which he set down on a small table near the bed without a word.

As the guard turned to leave, Tammie mustered her courage. "Wait!" she called out.

The guard paused but didn't turn around.

"Why am I here? What does Meliot want with me?"

The guard said nothing. He stepped out of the room, slamming the door behind him. The lock clicked into place, leaving Tammie alone once more.

Frustration bubbled up inside her. She wanted to scream, to demand answers, but she knew it would be useless. Whoever these people were, they weren't about to explain themselves to her.

Taking a deep breath, she walked over to the tray. There was bread, a bowl of stew, and a small jug of water. Her stomach growled at the delicious smell of the stew, but she ignored it. She didn't trust the food.

She went back to the wall and tapped twice. Erin responded immediately.

"Still here," Tammie said quietly. "We need to figure out a way to escape."

"It seems impossible," Erin replied. "There's a window in

my room, but the castle is too high on the cliff. We could easily plunge to our death. And the door is solid and reinforced with iron bars."

"Same here," Tammie muttered, glancing at her own window. "But if we're in adjoining rooms, maybe there's a way to break through the wall."

The idea sounded crazy, but it was the only thing she could come up with. If they could create a gap big enough to crawl through, they might have a chance of overpowering a guard or sneaking out.

"I don't know," Erin said doubtfully. "These walls are thick. It would take forever."

"Do you have anything heavy in your room?" Tammie asked, glancing around hers for anything she could use. "Like a chair or something?"

"Just the bed," Erin said. "It's made of wood, but it's too big to move."

Tammie sighed, frustration gnawing at her. Her only hope was that Niall, and the others would come to rescue them.

CHAPTER THIRTEEN

Niall had not planned to return to the other realm. Convinced that their curses were impossible to break, both he and Padriag had decided it was best to return to the keep and live out the rest of their days, which with Meliot's minions having overrun it, meant it could only a matter of days. For however long, at least they'd be in the familiar comfort of the home they'd known for hundreds of years.

It was only the strong sense of something being wrong that had brought him back. Tamara was in danger, and despite his decision, he could not allow harm to come to her. She'd put her life on hold, had worked tirelessly, and without his help, to free him.

Once materializing in Tristan's castle, he raced up the stairs to where her bedchamber was. He prayed she was asleep, and once he could reassure himself she was safe, he would return to the other alter-realm knowing she was unharmed.

The door was closed, the sense of foreboding grew, and his hand shook when turning the knob. Rushing into the room, he took in the rumpled bed. A covering had been pulled halfway off, most of it pooled on the rug. Rushing into the bathroom, he pushed the door open and took in the empty room.

"Tamara," he called out in a low tone, already knowing she would not respond.

Perhaps she'd waken and gone to eat, or ....

He moved to the bed leaned down hoping to get an idea of who had been there. Only her scent and that of love-making remained, but nothing else.

The window was wide open, the coolness of the room an obvious clue that that it had been like that for a long while.

"Niall. What happened?" Tristan and Gwen rushed into the room.

Gwen's wide eyes met his. "Where's my sister?"

Niall looked to Tristan for a beat before replying. "I have a feeling that Meliot had someone take her. I am fairly certain she was taken to the other realm."

Gwen rushed about the room, obviously searching for any clue. Upon entering the bathroom, she cried out. "Oh my god!"

Both he and Tristan peered into the tight space. Gwen pointed at the mirror. "She was taken."

She rushed to the night table and picked up what he knew to be some sort of communication device. "I'm calling Sabrina. They have to come back."

Tristan took the phone from her hand. "Neither she nor Gavin can travel to the alter-world. There is no need to worry her at this point. They are to return sometime today are they not?

Gwen nodded, not seeming at all convinced not to make the call.

Tristan took his wife into his arms and kissed the top of her head, his gaze meeting Niall's.

Niall turned to look at the open window. "I will return to Atlandia and recruit warriors to help with the rescue. I am sure the princesses will allow it. I will personally enlist Sterling's help as well," Niall said, referring to the princesses' brother, who'd tamed a dragon.

Gwen's tears were flowing freely down her face now. "Tamara is not prepared for this. She is not strong enough."

"Your sister is the most powerful of the three of you." Niall met Gwen's astonished gaze. "I have seen her powers firsthand. Although she is not in control of them, I have no doubt when the time comes, she will harness her strength."

Tristan's frustration was evident by the tightening of his jaw. "All of this is our fault. We should have accepted fate and remained in the other realm." His quiet words echoed what Niall had been thinking.

"I will not stop until Tamara is safe and back here with you."

Gwen let out a shaky breath "With you as her knight, I am reassured. Thank you, Niall."

Niall nodded, a knot forming in his throat. *Her knight.* For now he was, and he would save her no matter the cost.

"It is best I go. There is much to do." Niall took a step back.

"God speed to you and the others," Tristan told him.

"Liam will return with news." He dematerialized, going back to the other realm.

IT WAS LATE the next day when he'd finally been able to get permission to storm Meliot's castle. Argo the head guard, had managed to convince the princesses earlier that morning reports had come from the village that several women had gone missing in the night.

Liam, Padriag, and Niall waited impatiently as the leader of the shifters briefed the large contingency of warriors, both men who shifted into wolf form and those whose primary body was an actual wolf. Since they spoke in a combination of strange howls and a language he didn't understand, Niall could only decipher that they were divided into smaller groups and given an area where they'd enter the castle.

Finally, Argo walked toward them. "We leave at dawn," Argo said, his expression stern. The male exuded power and control. The shifter was formidable in battle and personally, Niall hoped never to have to fight against him.

"I have sent a messenger to Prince Sterling," Niall continued. "But I would not hold out much hope he will come. The Prince has issues on his own lands that require his constant attention."

"I think the messenger found him," Padriag said, his gaze moving past Argo's shoulder. "He is just now arriving."

The unmistakable sound of the beast broke through as the dragon came into view. It flew across the sky, seeming to float on the wind's currents, its attention aimed down.

With graceful swoops of expansive wings, Sterling's

dragon landed. The beast let out a loud roar, that sounded like an angry lion. With shimmering green, purple, and golden scales, and a long tail that swished from side to side, the dragon required a large space. The huge head turned as if taking in the area before it finally lowered close to the ground so that the prince could dismount.

Prince Sterling was a man befitting of his name. His hair, shimmered in the sun, a light ash blond, his eyes an unusual shade of silver. Niall was grateful for the man's presence, as the prince was rarely seen outside of his realm. As he walked toward them, his fur-lined gray cloak billowing from his shoulders and knee-high boots crunching on the ice, his unnatural silver gaze took them in.

"What, pray tell, is this urgent matter?" Stirling asked in a flat tone. "Let me forewarn you that neither my pet nor I will put our lives on the line for foolery."

Niall clenched his jaw. "I respectfully request you reconsider helping us Your Highness. In the darkness of night, village women were abducted and taken to Meliot's castle. Your help will ensure we can rescue them all."

Sterling looked off into the distance. Niall noticed a tick on the side of his face. "Why would Meliot take the women?"

What did it matter? Anger sizzled under Niall's skin, and it took all his strength to keep from shaking the man.

"Several women from the village are prisoners, and one woman from the other realm. Someone went there and took her."

Sterling's eyes snapped up at the mention of the woman's circumstance. "How is that possible?"

The prince turned back to the dragon. Niall wondered if

they communicated silently. When he faced them again, his face was expressionless. "Unfortunately, my hands are tied. My borders are vast, and I cannot afford a war with Meliot."

Niall glared at him. "Atlandia's warriors rides with us in the morning. Not only are your borders in jeopardy, but Atlandia's as well."

Sterling's expression didn't change. "There is more to this realm than Atlandia. My kingdom of Esland is too susceptible right now."

The three knights looked at each other, they'd never heard of a second kingdom. Niall locked gazes with the prince. "What of Middlesex? Are they not important? They lie on the border of the two lands."

"I do regret to hear about their misfortunes. But my hands are tied. I'd best go."

"Your Highness," Niall replied between clenched teeth.

The prince hesitated, his gaze looking past his shoulder toward the warriors who studied the dragon with fascination. "Godspeed to you all. I will assess my situation and return if I can." He turned on his heel and went back to the dragon.

Niall stalked toward the interior of the tent.

Padriag caught up with him. "That sucks. We sure could have used the assistance of a dragon."

"We will succeed with or without a dragon," Niall replied.

"I believe we will," Liam added stepping up on the other side of him.

"Yeah," Padriag finished pumping a fist in the air. "Nobody takes our woman and lives."

. . .

DAWN CAME. Niall had not slept because he was worried about Tamara and because he wanted to avoid Devina.

Once dressed and having eaten a surprisingly hearty breakfast of eggs, crusty bread and fried pork, he headed out to find his steed.

Upon seeing him, the horse pawed the ground, his huge hoof making deep impressions. Niall stroked the horse's mane. "Today we will be victorious, friend. Tomorrow you and I will return to the keep."

He glanced upwards, the third moon was new, a sliver in the sky. Once it became a full moon, the days would never be bright but remained in a twilight. The suns were barely above the horizon, giving an eerie glow to the surroundings.

The warriors were in the process of mounting, each male heavily armed with swords strapped to their backs, daggers across the chest, and more weaponry about their waists and on the saddles.

Niall mounted and double checked to ensure he'd not forgotten anything. Liam and Padriag pulled their horses alongside him. The warriors lined up in two rows, Argo in the lead. A gigantic warrior, Argo's first to his right, signaled for the force to move forward.

The horses moved at a brisk pace, several wolves running alongside. The huge silver and brown wolves kept up with the horses with ease.

Niall often wondered about sentinels. Although they could shift to human form, they seemed to prefer wolf form to fight. Shifters, like Argo, on the other hand were more at home in human form. He studied the warrior's large frame and didn't doubt the shifter would bring terror to anyone he confronted.

He glanced to Liam who scowled, his gaze forward.

"Is there something we should worry about?" he asked the stoic Brit.

Liam's frosty blue eyes settled on him. "I do not have a clear vision, just chaos. I am trying my best to conjure a stronger picture but am finding it difficult."

Niall's eyebrows shot up. "That's not reassuring."

"It is not." Liam shook his head. "Hopefully I will get some insight before we arrive. Right now, it's not clear enough for me to foretell."

"I pray it is so," Niall replied, noticing Liam's troubled look remained. "Is there something else Liam?"

"Whatever you're planning. It will not come to be. You will not live at the keep."

Damn the man's gift.

"I've got enough to worry about without you planning to kill yourself." Liam hissed.

"What are you two talking about?" Padriag asked from behind him. "Who's going to kill himself?"

"No one," both answered at the same time.

Padriag grunted. "Then why did you say it, Liam?"

Liam gave Niall a warning look. "I am telling Niall that he needs to follow Argo's orders. You do as well. I know his women are in there, but he doesn't allow his heart to overrule his brains."

Unsure what Liam meant, Niall remained silent. Whatever they discovered in the castle would affect him. Especially if Tamara was injured or worse.

"Argo better have a good plan," Padriag replied.

Soon they would arrive at the castle. So far they'd not come across any sentinels. It didn't mean Meliot wasn't aware of their arrival. The wizard had eyes and ears everywhere. To think they would take him by surprise was not smart. Sooner rather than later, they would encounter the first of what could be many obstacles.

THE WOODS BECAME THICKER and darker. Padriag cast a spell that illuminated the way. Argo turned and glared at him. "Dim the illumination, we can see in the dark."

"We are not shifters and can't," Padriag informed him.

"Your horses can," Argo replied. "Besides, there are three moons, once we arrive at a clearing, the night is bright."

"Dim them," Niall told the rebellious knight. "I can see well enough."

The lights went out. Niall blinked. He couldn't see a thing and hoped that, indeed, his horse could.

A break in the woods gave way to a clearing. As Argo predicted, they were able to see well. Meliot's lands seemed to be in perpetual dusk, no moons, no suns, just a hazy light of a stormy looking sky. Niall looked up for a moment at the display.

Argo pulled his horse around and waited for the guard to line up before him. "My strongest warrior and I will shift and take these." He held what looked like ropes with hooks on the ends. "Niall and Padriag will scale the wall and enter on the second level." He turned to Liam. "You will lead the wolves through the front gates to create a distraction."

Liam nodded, and the sentinels bowed their heads in acknowledgment.

Argo raised his hand to get his attention. "When you hear my whistle, retreat. Now go to your appointed places."

"How are we to leave with the women?" Niall asked.

Argo met his gaze for a moment. "My first and I will assist. You must rappel back to the ground with the women."

"Right." Padriag looked as puzzled as Niall felt. "Easy peasy, grab the women, somehow make it to the wall, and then rappel down. I am sure it will work. Not a problem." What Padriag said echoed his thoughts, and yet, he would take the chance, do what he must to save Tamara.

Argo's shrug wasn't reassuring. "Is there another way?"

Without warning, Argo and his first turned into huge birds of prey. The ropes in their claws, the birds soared toward the sky.

"I didn't know they could do that," Padriag said, awe in his voice as he craned his neck to follow the birds. "Maybe they should go into the rooms. Makes more sense."

With a rumble of growls, Liam and the sentinels charged forward,

Warriors in human form charged on their horses, some behind the wolves, others splitting into two groups going to opposite sides of the castle.

"This is going to be fun," Padriag said as he and Niall went to find where the ropes would be.

By the sounds of clashing swords and screams, the sentinels and warriors had entered the courtyard.

Two thick ropes unfurled down the stone wall. Grabbing the ends, Niall and Padriag jumped from their steeds and began the climb to the narrow windows. The large birds of prey's flapping wings assured their backs were covered.

Finally Niall reached a thin window. The wooden shutter was closed so he kicked it in and squeezed through the opening. It was barely wide enough for him to fit through.

Inside Tamara jerked up to sit on the bed, holding a wine goblet up over her head, probably the only thing she could find to use as a weapon.

"It is me," he whispered, pulling the cloak collar down so she could see his face.

"I knew you would come," Tamara cried out, flinging herself into his arms, wrapping hers around his neck. Her entire body shook. "I have never been so scared in my life." Her body against his made him feel ten times stronger. That she was terrified only served to fan the flames of fury that overtook him.

"I think Meliot is planning something horrible tonight. We have to save the others." She tugged him toward the front door.

"We cannot go that way." He pulled her toward the window. "He probably has guards posted outside the door."

She gave him a pleading look and leaned into this ear to whisper. "We can't leave the woman in the other room. Her name is Erin. She is trapped in the room next to mine. She is also from the other realm."

He urged her closer to the window and motioned to Padriag to go into the next room. Then picked her up. "Padriag will get her."

"What of the other women?" Tamara asked as they made their way to the window.

Just as Niall was about to answer, the door burst open, two beastly guards came into the room.

Moving Tamara behind his back, Niall pulled his sword. "Go through the window, grab the rope and tie it around your waist. Hold tight."

He swung his sword at the approaching guards who moved forward warily.

A thick mist spread across the floor engulfing the room. It was impossible to see anything, so Niall continued to swing his sword wildly.

"I find it amusing that you thought you could just waltz in and take my guests." The mists parted and Meliot entered the room. Immediately the shutters on the window slammed shut.

The wizard eyed Niall then his gaze slid to Tamara, who had ignored his instructions to get out and clung to the back of his shirt. "I have been waiting a long time to meet you."

Still behind him, but peeking out, Tamara gasped but remained silent.

The wizard shrugged. "All will be clear soon enough." Cupping his hands together, he formed a fireball, the blue flames moving like live snakes. "Your protector will have to die. You will thank me when you understand the destiny that awaits you."

Just as he flung it, Tamara held her hands straight in front of her, palms facing the wizard. The fireball seemed to bounce at coming in contact with her hands and ricocheted back hitting the wizard. He took a step back, his expression accessing her.

"Let us go," Tamara's voice shook.

The wizard narrowed his eyes. "You are not trained, you cannot control your powers." He turned to the guards. "Kill them."

Shuffling and cursing, Padriag and a woman were dragged into the room. Padriag was unarmed, but he didn't seem injured. The woman, a slender brunette, clung to his side.

Padriag yelled out a protection spell, creating an invisible shield. It would not stand long against Meliot, but it would give them time.

"Go to the window now!" Niall told Padriag. "Take the women with you."

The wizard cocked his head to one side, as if amused by them and then looked to his guards. "I said kill them."

The beastly guards rushed forward crashing through Padriag's shield that no doubt had been weakened by Meliot.

When they were but mere inches from them, Tamara held out both hands casting what he could only describe as pulses of energy. It sent the guards tumbling backward. The downed beasts shuddered, their limbs curled unnaturally. The screams left no doubt that they were in agony.

The entire time, an expression of pride spread across Meliot's face.

The respite didn't last. The wizard flicked his right-hand, sending Niall and Padriag flying across the room, crashing against the wall. Niall managed to keep hold of his sword, but upon collapsing to the floor, all air left his body.

The wizard had him in a vice like hold, the grip so tight, he couldn't draw air into his lungs. Despite struggling, he couldn't free himself. By the sound of Padriag's gasps, he suffered the same hold.

"Stop, you're killing them," Tamara screamed. She pushed pulse after pulse toward the wizard. It was ineffective. Meliot was much too powerful.

"Help them," the other woman screamed.

Darkness ebbed as Niall did his best to suck in air, but it was useless. When a pulse of energy struck him, the vice eased just enough he could draw breath. He prayed the same happened to Padriag.

A second energy pulse struck, and the hold around them was gone. Niall tried to stand, but the best he could do was get on his hands and knees.

More guards had arrived, one after another going toward Tamara, only to fall. It was obvious she was tiring. Niall managed to yank a dagger and fling it at a guard just as he almost reached her. The blade sunk into his neck and the creature fell to his knees and disintegrated.

"I've had enough." Meliot held up his hands forming a shield as he walked closer to Tamara. "Accept your destiny. This is your home now." He glanced to Niall and Padriag, who remained too weak to fight.

"Take them to the dungeon." Enormous guards neared and grabbed Niall by the arm, dragging him to his feet. Even if he'd had his full strength, Niall couldn't fight four huge warriors.

Once out of the room, Niall pulled a dagger and stabbed one of them in the side, the beastly being grunted, but didn't release him. Again and again, he sunk the blade into the now bloody flesh, until finally the guard collapsed.

The guard on his other side grabbed his wrist, preventing him from stabbing him and Niall kneed him as hard as he could between the legs. By the squeal it let out and the way he fell face-first onto the wooden flooring, the beasts had the same vulnerable spot as other males. He leaned over the guard and sliced its throat.

Flinging a dagger into the nape of one of the beasts that had Padriag sent that guard falling onto the floor. Taking advantage of the distraction, quick as lightening, Padriag dispatched the fallen guard as Niall attacked the other one by jumping on its back and slicing his sharpened blade across its throat.

Niall signaled for Padriag to follow him back to the room where Tamara and the other woman were. They stopped just outside, unsure how to proceed.

Meliot seemed to be growing impatient. "Stop fighting me and accept your fate." A grunt told Niall that Tamara continued to fight the wizard, and for whatever reason, Meliot seemed unable to fight her.

They'd suspected he'd been growing weaker, as the quests he'd sent them on in the last year had become less perilous and his skin had taken an ashen hue as of late.

"Enough with the fate shit. I am not staying here. You are not killing my friends, and I am going to ensure you never harm anyone again." Tamara's voice was tight with anger, but the slight tremor told Niall she was terrified. "You are a terrible villain. Do you know why?"

When Meliot didn't respond, she continued. "Because you cannot kill any of us. Something blocks you from it. I am right aren't I?"

Niall smiled in spite of himself. He loved her spunk.

He loved her.

The wizard sneered. "You will worship me, once you discover the powers within. I am your sire, therefore darkness lives within you."

It had to be a lie. There was nothing dark within Tamara. Niall prayed she didn't believe him.

"Ha," Tamara replied. "That I don't believe. If I was in anyway related to you, I would sense it. The only thing I feel for you is hate."

Sounds of battle became louder. The sentinels and Atlandian warriors had managed to get inside the castle.

Niall hoped with all his might they'd get to them in time.

Chapter Fourteen

The wizard was not her father. Despite feeling assured that he lied, a part of her wondered if that could be the reason her mother was so against her going to Scotland.

Tammie's entire body felt as if she had her hand around an electric wire. Everything tingled but it wasn't unpleasant. Somehow she knew it was a power that she needed to harness, to control if she and the others were to have a chance of escape.

The wizard, Meliot, was just as she'd pictured him. Long lack-luster silver hair hung limp past his shoulders. He wore robing that was belted with what looked to be a golden cord. He was not an ugly man, but the malevolence he exuded made him terrifying.

His eyes were as black as night when he studied her. "Save your strength, you are not strong enough to stand against me."

"Come in. I know you are there," Meliot said, glancing over his shoulder. "This is my realm. I know all, see all."

Hands bound Niall and Padriag appeared in the doorway, both had been stripped of their weapons, and were flanked by four of the beastlike guards.

Tammie pulled energy inward and considered how to strike the guards that held Niall and Padriag, but she wasn't sure enough of her aim.

"Bring them," Meliot instructed sweeping from the room. The guards walked forward, dragging a struggling Niall and Padriag with them.

Niall turned met her gaze and mouthed. "Run."

She mouthed "No," back. She wasn't about to leave them there.

Although she didn't doubt that Meliot could inflict harm, to the point of them wishing for death, his lack of response earlier confirmed her suspicions.

The Wizard couldn't kill them.

When she and Erin stepped past the doorway, they caught sight of the men turning a corner.

"I don't know what to do," Erin said in a trembling voice. The woman's skin was pale, her eyes red. "I am still not sure why I am here. We need to escape, run." Her voice lowered to a whisper.

"We can't. The wizard will send those things after us. I have to find out where they went, and your best bet is to stay with me. I'm sorry," Tammie said as they took off at a jog in hopes of finding out where Meliot had taken Niall and Padriag.

The castle was a labyrinth of corridors, doorways, and

empty rooms. Some led to open spaces, others to balconies from which the expanse of a dark forest could be viewed.

Just as Tammie was about to give up, they entered what looked to be a throne room of sorts.

Heart in her throat, Tammie moved into the space slowly, stopping at seeing Meliot. The wizard had his back to her, but he was aware she was there.

Other than a blazing fire in a monstrosity of a fireplace, there was no other lighting in the room.

Niall and Padriag had been chained to a wall. Neither struggled. They were either held still by magic, or aware it would be useless.

Meliot turned to face her. "You are right, daughter mine. I cannot kill them, as much as I would love to. They have caused me more grief as of late than they're worth."

A shiver of revulsion traveled down Tammie's spine at him referring to her as his daughter. "Then let them go. Stop all this. They have more than paid the price for whatever trespass you perceive they did. Enough."

The maniac shook his head, giving her a look like that of a parent to a petulant child. "It is not in my nature to do so. No, what I will do instead is to send them to a place where neither you nor anyone else will ever find them."

"No!" Tammie screamed.

"You are right about one thing," Meliot continued. "It is enough."

"What is this Meliot?" A lithe, tall, dark-haired woman stepped through the doorway, her eyes trained on Niall the entire time. "I wasn't aware you entertained. Why wasn't I invited?"

An aura of darkness surrounded the woman and Tammie immediately recognized her. This was the woman in the dream. The one who tortured Niall.

Meliot's gaze swept over the woman. "This is not the time, Devina."

Instead of replying she walked around the wizard directly to where Niall stood. "Why is he here?"

All color drained from Niall's face, but he didn't look at the woman, instead his eyes were fixed on Meliot.

"The knights came to rescue the damsels in distress," Meliot informed her in a bored tone. "Why are you here?"

"Damsels?" Devina whirled around obviously noticing Tammie and Erin for the first time.

Tammie did her best to tamp down her fear, although she suspected the thundering of her heart was obvious.

Devina's eyes narrowed, her head cocked to the side as she stalked toward her. "Who are you?" She took a step closer to Tammie and studied her. "Do I know you?"

"I sired her. Her magic is already strong. I would maintain my distance." The pride in Meliot's voice made Tammie cringe. "She has come to claim her birthright and will rule the land, she will be more powerful that you and I combined."

Niall's eyes widened.

Tammie fought to keep the fear at bay.

She locked gazes with Niall. She heard his thoughts. *I failed you.*

Not yet you haven't.

Devina caught the exchange between them and moved closer to her. She leaned forward and sniffed at her.

"Ah yes, I do know you." Her face twisted into a rage as she slid a look to Meliot. "She is not that powerful. I am sure you are mistaken. The one you sired is not her."

For the first time since meeting Meliot, he seemed unsure. "What do you speak of?"

When Devina didn't reply, he flew at her, curling his pale long fingers around her throat. "What. Do. You. Know." He pronounced each word slowly, deliberately.

The woman fought against the hold, her hands clawing at his. Tammie took advantage of the distraction and rushed to Niall. Curling her fingers around the chains, she concentrated energy in an attempt to break them.

The chains loosened enough that Niall slipped his hand out from the manacles. Quickly she did the same with Padriag.

When she looked to the door, Niall, tapped her arm and whispered. "Wait."

She moved away from him just as Meliot released his hold on Devina, the demon gasped in air, her face contorted in anger.

"She was sired for a specific purpose. However, her fate is locked with yours, however. Perhaps a slave... who cares." Devina whirled toward Tammie. "I doubt she will be agreeable. You will have a fight on your hands."

Devina stalked to Tammie and lifted her hand as if to slap her, but before she could Tammie managed to hurl a blast of energy at the demon so hard that she stumbled backwards falling onto the stone floor.

With an enraged scream, Devina lunged at her, only to be intercepted by Niall, who got the brunt of the hit and was hurled back against the wall he'd been chained to.

Tammie was in a fight once. A girl in middle school called her a bitch, and before she thought better of it, she'd knocked the girl to the ground and began to pound her. Memories came flying back when Devina rushed at her, fingernails aimed at her face. They tumbled to the floor, Devina screeching and Tammie punching her as hard as she could.

Tammie was able to throw the woman off to the side and jump to her feet. Just as she got her footing, the woman rushed toward her again.

Enough was enough. Tammie harnessed all the anger and fear and threw a fireball at the advancing woman. It was as if the demon was electrocuted. She shook violently before falling to the floor where she was still.

BEFORE TAMMIE COULD CELEBRATE any kind of victory, an invisible vise surrounded her, pinning her arms to her sides. How long would this continue? This going back and forth, or more appropriately, one step forward and several back?

Niall and Padriag were being held by the guards, although struggling, it was evident they, too, were tiring.

Exhaustion poured from her and Tammie fought tears. She wouldn't cry. This was not a time to show any kind of weakness.

The room was silent, and she could barely draw a breath, the hold was paralyzing.

Of the two things, whether she was Meliot's daughter, or she was to be his slave of sorts, neither was an acceptable option. Demons always lied. Devina had to have lied to distract Meliot, so she could attempt to kill her.

The room seemed to tilt. He was trying to put her in a trance. Tammie clenched her eyes closed and forced her hand upwards. A weak fireball hit the wizard. He flinched but did not release her.

"Let her go." The threat in Niall's voice seemed to affect Meliot more than her fireball. The hold on Tammie loosened when the wizard whirled around to face the knight.

"You can never win against me. Accept your fate. You will be in another realm until your dying breath. Never will you see the place you lived before."

Meliot picked up one of the discarded swords and advanced toward Niall and Padriag.

Niall glanced at her. *Go now.*

Tammie realized the hold on her had loosened even more.

She looked at Erin and motioned for her to go toward the door.

Erin shook her head. Like her, either because of fear or because she, too, was not leaving Niall and Padriag with the madman and his idiot guards.

Sword in hand, Meliot advanced toward Niall.

In desperation, Tammie pulled as much power as she could draw from everything in her surroundings and formed a large fireball. Just as Meliot drew up the large sword, she flung it at him with all her might.

The wizard stumbled, and the sword fell out of his hand clanging against the hard stone floor.

Both Niall and Padriag fought anew, but were no match for the stronger, larger creatures that held them in place.

Suddenly an explosion shook the castle, the sound so loud, every occupant in the room scrambled toward the interior wall. The entire exterior wall disintegrated. Stones flew in all directions. Tammie and Erin rushed for cover under a table.

The guards seemed to know what happened as all six men drew swords and advanced toward the large gaping hole.

Fire projected through the opening, and they jumped back.

Whoomp. Whoomp. Whoomp. The sound of large wings preceded another blast of fire. Two of the beast-like guards fell dead, a third rolled on the ground attempting to put out the flames crawling over him.

Meliot rushed towards her and Erin and grabbed them by the arms. "Come we must go or perish."

Tammie yanked her arm away. "I am not going anywhere with you."

Erin kicked at the wizard. He slapped her hard, and she fell against the wall and slid down, unconscious.

He went to pick her up. Tammie jumped on his back pounding and kicking him.

A force threw her off, and she landed with a loud thump. Tammie rolled away to avoid being stepped on by a guard that fought whatever it was that came in through the opening. When he burned and crumpled to the floor, the last guard dropped his sword and ran out of the room.

What she saw next made her mouth fall open.

A dragon.

A real dragon.

She stumbled backwards. The beast's shimmering eyes glanced over her before they locked on Meliot who blasted it with a fireball. The dragon leaped. avoiding a direct hit with agility that shocked her.

Huge talons wrapped around the wizard pinning his arms to the sides. Meliot's struggles were futile. The huge beast flapped its wings and turned midair heading away from the castle.

"You'll pay for this, Sterling," Meliot threatened as the dragon disappeared into the sky with the screaming wizard in his claws.

The man Meliot had called Sterling stood in the middle of the room with what looked to Tammie like a bored expression. His long silver-blonde hair whipped around his striking face, the ends waved in the wind. "Help me." He motioned to Niall and Padriag, and together the men shoved the larger stones against the door.

Then he picked up the still unconscious Erin, and motioned to Tammie and the others. "When Dragos returns you will leave."

Tammie opened her mouth to protest, but the dragon appeared as suddenly as the first time.

The man looked toward the knights, "Come let us go before more guards arrive. The stones will not hold them off for long."

"Some assistance would be nice," Padriag replied, holding up his bound hands.

"Yes, of course," the male somehow managed to keep Erin in his arms and swing his sword, breaking through the bounds with a graceful swing.

Niall grabbed Tammie's hand, and as a group they hurried to the large beast that had lowered itself to allow them to climb on his back.

"What exactly do I hold on to?" Tammie asked. She tried to swallow, but her throat was dry. "I'm afraid of heights."

When Padriag mounted, Sterling handed Erin to him and stood back.

"Your help saved us," Niall told the blonde male who watched them with what seemed to be a bored expression on his face.

It was then that Devina sat up dazed, when she spotted them on the dragon, she shrieked and tried to lift her hand to throw a fireball, but Sterling stopped her. He grabbed her arms and pulled them behind her, holding her in place.

"Eeeeeeeeek!" Tammie couldn't stop from screaming when the dragon leaped into the air. Tammie held on to the nearest scale, her knuckles turning white as she hung on for dear life.

The beast began to descend, and Tammie looked to Niall who held her against him. "Why are we landing so soon?"

"We are too heavy, besides he has to return for Sterling," Niall informed her.

The beast lighted onto the ground. Astounded by the beast's grace, Tammie didn't think to protest when Niall carried her into the woods. She watched over his shoulder to see the dragon take flight again toward Meliot's castle.

"Do you think that Sterling guy is going to be all right?"

"Sterling can take care of himself." Niall replied.

Snow fell onto the frozen ground. Tammie snuggled against Niall as he carried her, using his cloak to keep them both warm. She tried to protest, insisting that she was perfectly capable of walking, but he'd told her this way they could both use the cloak and share body warmth.

They walked for almost an hour before the men finally walked into a clearing and stopped.

Padriag and Erin dematerialized.

"Are you taking me back to Scotland?"

"Yes."

"Will you return?"

"Close your eyes and hold on to me," Niall told her.

Not wanting a repeat of what happened last time with Gunther, she did.

"You're back!" Gwen's voice was the first thing Tammie heard as they appeared inside the McRainey estate. "Thank God." Her sister and husband rushed to them.

Everyone moved to the library where Padriag lay Erin down on the coach. The girl started to come to, and Padriag kissed her face, relieved. The young knight looked around the room. "She's okay, just took a knock to the head."

Gwen frowned at Tammie. "I think both of you need to see a doctor. You have bruises on your face."

Tammie touched her jaw. It did hurt, and she reached for a throw and wrapped it around her shoulders as the coldness of Atlandia lingered in her body.

Niall had moved away from her and stood next to the fireplace. She sensed him distancing himself.

They answered as many questions as they could, each taking turns to talk. Tammie did most of the talking, while Niall sulked and Padriag hovered over Erin, who was slowly coming to. She blinked in confusion, remaining silent as Tammie told the others all that had happened after being taken by Gunther.

Gavin walked in with beers and handed one to Tristan, Padriag, and the still-sullen Niall. Sabrina poured wine for the women, and they drank whilst discussing the situation. If it weren't for the situation, one would think it was a normal night with friends hanging out.

Padriag lowered himself to the couch to sit next to Erin. He seemed to have taken his role as her protector very seriously.

"What about Liam?" Tammie asked not looking at Niall.

"I am going to return to check on him," Niall replied. Of course he'd be the first to volunteer to go back. Tammie bit her lip to keep from asking if he planned to come back.

"I can go," Padriag told them, I have to see what happens there. Soon the three moons will be high in the sky.

"What does that mean?" Erin asked.

"They have been trapped in that world. Each has a specific curse that must be broken," Gwen explained.

"Three lives rescued, upon three moons high. Two hearts restored. One must die." Tammie said out loud. "There were three lives rescued today. The three moons were there. I don't know about the rest."

"Or who must die," Niall finished for her. "Either Liam or I will return with news." His eyes remained trained on her, but he didn't move any closer.

"Padriag will return with news," Tammie interrupted, but he was already gone.

Indeed the knight had vanished.

Tristan placed a hand on Niall's shoulder. "You should wait, Niall. Remain here tonight. Let's wait and see what news Padriag brings.

What about Niall's curse? How would it be broken? The more Tammie pondered the words of his spell, the more confused she became.

THE HOURS PASSED with no news. Tristan and Gwen had gone to the kitchen to make more coffee. Tammie nodded but jerked awake at the silence of the room.

Where was Niall?

Erin was on the love seat reading the spell book. Her eyes constantly darting to the doorway.

Tammie stood and stretched. "Did you see where Niall went?"

"No," Erin replied. "But he was yawning earlier. He may be asleep somewhere." She stretched. "The groundskeeper, Miles, is taking me home. I need to sleep, and then I will return to see what I can do to help. If I was taken to the other realm, it must mean I am connected to this."

Tammie went to the woman. "I am grateful that you were there, that we were able to help each other."

"I am packing in the morning and going to stay with my aunt and uncle. They live not too far from here. I feel safer not to be in my flat alone."

"Good idea," Tammie said. "Make sure you rest."

Erin hugged her just as Miles, appeared in the driveway. "Are you ready Miss?"

· · ·

DECIDING TO FIND NIALL, Tammie walked with Erin and Miles to the front door. Once they left, she went to the kitchen where only Tristan and Gwen sat at the table. They were playing cards. Both looked up as she approached.

"Just walking around, don't want to go to sleep."

Gwen smiled at her warmly. "Tammie go lie down. When Padriag and Liam appear, I will come and wake you. Tristan and I got plenty of rest, we'll remain awake."

It was true, she was exhausted. Tammie climbed to the second floor, deciding that once she found Niall, she'd sleep for a couple hours.

From the hallway, she peeked into one of the spare bedrooms. Hearing noises, she darted into the next room and found Niall on the bed. He was asleep, his head tossed from side to side. He seemed to be dreaming. She touched his shoulder. "Niall? Are you all right?"

He jerked, but did not wake. When he mumbled incoherently, she became alarmed and shook him. "Niall wake up."

Again he jerked, but did not wake. Tammie touched his forehead, it was hot, feverish. At her touch he turned his face into her hand. She stroked his face in an attempt to sooth him.

Was he in Devina's realm? Tammie lowered to sit on the edge of the bed and closed her eyes, attempting to seek answers.

ONE MINUTE he'd been in the library, the next he'd found himself in a bedroom. He'd fought against whatever force drove him there, but it was strong. When he'd been flung on the bed and held down. He continued to fight. But finally, the fatigue and lack of sleep was too much of an invincible foe and he succumbed.

Now, as expected, he was back in Devina's dungeon. The vile woman standing in front of him holding a dagger she'd heated over the fire.

Chained to the wall he could only wait to see what creative methods of torture she'd use this time.

"I won't heal your wounds this time, Niall," Devina told him, holding the dagger against his stomach. He clenched his teeth at the pain. The smell of his own burning flesh made his stomach turn. Devina stepped back. "Did that hurt lover?"

As usual, he refused to speak to her. What did it matter? Many years, no matter what he did or said, because he refused to give himself to her, he'd still been tortured. She got pleasure from seeing him beaten.

"You knew that if you fucked that bitch, you'd pay. Yet you did it anyway," Devina told him, her voice laced with venom. "I'm going to make you wish you were dead. Then I'm going to kill her."

He'd die before allowing Devina to hurt Tamara. Rage surged, and he fought not to react. She'd enjoy it too much.

Devina continued. "First she will see you as deformed as I leave you, and she will be repelled by you. How will you deal with that?"

She went to a table and picked up a long steel rod. "I'm not sure what to do with this." A guard stepped up and whispered to her. Devina laughed at whatever he said and studied the rod. "Broken knees are not that exciting."

A whip got her attention; she held it up and smiled. "I do love the sound of a lashing."

She raised the whip and swung, welts formed across his chest as the leather throngs tore into his flesh. He winced but did not cry out. Soon the pain would grow so large he'd become feverish, incoherent and not feel at all. He glared at Devina who swung again, this time she aimed for his face.

Suddenly the whip flew out of Devina's hand.

Tamara stood in the room.

Surely this was an illusion.

Devina stumbled backward, surprised to see her there. "How are you here?" She grabbed a dagger from the table and flung it at Tamara. It bounced off an invisible protective shield.

Tamara lifted her hand and threw a fireball at Devina, sending the woman flying against a wall. The two guards present rushed toward Tamara but could not get close to her as a wall of blue fire came up from the floor blocking their path.

His chains fell off his wrists and ankles. Niall fell forward but caught himself before collapsing onto the ground.

Come.

He heard Tamara's call and moved toward her, hesitating at the firewall.

"No!" Devina screamed tossing a knife in the air toward him, he dodged it and jumped through the fire.

Tamara grabbed his hand. "Now wake up."

Niall jerked awake. He sprang up to see Tamara watching him from a chair next to the bed.

She didn't say anything, but her eyes locked onto his chest.

The lash marks remained. Lifting the sheet, he saw that the red fresh burn mark on his stomach also stayed.

"I'll go get something for that." Tamara stood and went to the doorway.

"You are trapped in two cages. The one by Meliot and the one by Devina."

She placed a paper on the bed and walked out.

He picked it up. It was a poem or a spell. He didn't understand the words, so he read them again.

One of the valiant will once again live
Call to the end of the rising of darkness
The powers of evil diminishing
Lights of three moons shining above
The keys to two cages are sacrifice and love

He frowned at the words.

"John McMurray sent it." Tristan leaned on the doorway. "He is Liam's partner. Owns a bookstore in Edinburgh."

"What does it have to do with me?" Niall asked, getting up from the bed, flinching at the pain it caused.

Tristan's eyes locked to his. "Your enchantment called for a master of pages. Remember?"

Spell of ages from Master of pages. Sacrifice fate for the knight in two cages.

Niall shrugged. "I suppose so. How is this McMurray a master of any kind?"

"He is also a mystic. Liam's love."

His shoulders slumped, he should have left and returned to the other realm. Now he had to tell Tristan he would not allow his own rescue.

The laird went to stand by the window and gazed outside as if deep in thought. "It's been over three hundred years, Niall. I have known you for over three centuries. I can almost read your thoughts." Tristan's troubled green eyes met his. "You have your reasons for not wanting to leave, for not giving us the chance to help free you. Until Tamara, I'd pretty much given up on trying to convince you to tell us the rules of breaking your enchantment. But you told her."

His words cut through him, and he had a difficult time meeting his friend's gaze.

Tristan continued. "A small part of you must have wanted to be saved if you did that."

"It is only because I know how impossible it is that I told her. She kept asking. The lass is relentless." He pressed his lips together to hold back the proud smile that threatened. "I can never be truly free Tristan."

His friend shook his head. "Nothing is impossible, Niall. I will never give up. We will never give up. You're my brother."

A lump formed in his throat, and he wished he could give Tristan hope.

"It will break her heart. I hope you are prepared ..." Tristan stopped talking as Tammie entered the room. She held a small box under her arm.

She eyed each of them in turn. "What happens?

"He'll tell you," Tristan replied and gave Niall one last concerned look before walking out.

Tammie pushed him back onto the bed. She began to cleanse the wounds. Her face serene, she didn't speak the entire time as she rubbed ointment on them and placed bandages over the deeper lash cuts. She put a cooling substance over the burn. "You should probably walk around shirtless for a while and allow it to get fresh air. Burns heal faster that way." Her voice strained.

He grabbed her hand. "Tamara look at me."

Her eyes glistened with unshed tears when they lifted to his. She sniffed and wiped at an errant tear with her arm. "How long has she been hurting you? I can't believe someone can be so evil."

He didn't reply, instead pulled her into his arms and held her. Niall inhaled the lavender smell of her hair and closed his eyes. It would be hard to leave, but no matter what, he could not subject her to the horrible truth that was his life. "It's not always so bad," he lied.

She lifted her face to him. "I don't think I believe you."

Her lips parted and he covered them with his, lacking the power to keep from it. When she pushed her tongue into his mouth to explore, he cupped her face.

Her hands slid down his body, avoiding his injuries. Light yet firm caresses were a piece of heaven.

They held each other, not speaking. He had to tell her goodbye. It was probably better if he left sooner rather than later.

Tammie met his eyes. "Tell me what this means." She

lifted the paper with the spell and read it out loud. "*One of the valiant will once again live. Call to the end of the rising of darkness. The powers of evil diminishing. Lights of three moons shining above. The keys to the cages are sacrifice and love.*"

He lifted her face up to look at him. "Those words do not matter. I have to go."

Shoulders slumping, Tammie nodded. "Fine. I won't try to stop you Niall. I don't know what else I can do." Her voice was too calm. His chest squeezed at seeing her so defeated.

He got up and carefully dressed, not looking at her.

Without a word, she walked out of the room leaving him alone. Then he closed his eyes and willed himself back to the alter-world.

Nothing happened.

Chapter Sixteen

Padriag appeared near the caves. Argo looked up as he neared, the shifter's expression harsher than usual.

"Did anyone get hurt?" Padriag asked him.

"Two of our guardsmen are injured, one badly. They've been taken back to Atlandia. We are about to head there ourselves." Argo looked away toward the woods. "The villagers of Middlesex cannot survive without protection. The Princesses have decreed that they all relocate closer to the castle. At least until their numbers increase, then they can request permission to reestablish the village."

"Are we going to help them?"

Argo shook his head. "Half of the guard left early this morning. They are probably arriving at the castle soon."

Padriag hesitated before asking, hoping his friend was not one of the injured. "Is Liam here?"

"Yes. He just returned shortly." Argo motioned to the caves. "He's packing."

Returned? "Thank you, I'll go retrieve my belongings as well." Padriag ran up the hill.

The guardsmen were mounting and preparing to leave, and head back to Atlandia.

"Where the hell have you been?" Padriag yelled storming into the tent.

Liam tightened the strap on the bundle he kneeled next to and looked up. "Where the hell have *you* been?" he asked in return, emphasizing the word 'you.' He went back to picking up the remaining items. "I thought I would end up taking the three horses back to the castle myself. Where's Niall?"

"He's still back in the other realm." Padriag began to pick up his belongings. "How will he know where to find us? Maybe I should take the horses, and you go and tell him to return to the castle."

The sounds of hooves interrupted their conversation. Liam headed towards the tent entrance. "Come on, we still have to saddle the horses and catch up."

Snow wasn't falling, but the air remained frigid. Padriag let out a puff of air as he went after Liam. The ugliness of the frozen land mirrored his mood. "Liam wait," he called after the Brit, who'd reached one of the horses. "You never answered my question."

A slow coloring, followed by a wide smile told more than Liam's words. "I went to Edinburgh. Popped in to visit John."

"Oh, well shit. That's great," Padriag replied truthfully. "I was beginning to wonder if you'd lost interest, you haven't seen him in a long time."

Padriag tied his bag and bedroll onto Niall's horse's saddle. "It's nice to know that you, Gavin, and Tristan found happiness."

Liam walked over and stood directly in front of him. "Something is wrong. Why are you saying only the three of us?"

Not sure he wanted to have the conversation, Padriag shrugged. "My time is over, nothing happened. Three lives were rescued. Niall, Erin and Tammie. I don't know about hearts restored. Maybe that's you and John. No one died, which is a good thing."

"The moons are in the sky," Liam pointed out. "It is not over yet." The Brit went to his horse. "If we don't hurry, we'll never catch up with the guard."

They mounted and began the trek back toward the castle riding side-by-side, with Niall's horse following behind.

Padriag looked at Liam. "You should go now. It's time to allow yourself time with John, time to be happy. To be free of all this. Niall and I will find our destiny whether it's here or in the other realm."

"Why the sudden pessimism?" Liam frowned at him. "I gave my word. I will remain and help you."

Humbled at Liam's nobility, Padriag tried to think of the words needed to allow Liam to leave without it seeming as if he'd given up on them. It shamed him to think that of all the men he'd spent the last three hundred plus years with, Liam was the one he'd never been close to. Liam always maintained a distance. Possibly his upbringing in the English aristocracy caused him to seem like that. Either way, he should have gotten to know the man who obviously cared very much for him and Niall.

"I'm sorry Liam." Padriag started and had to clear his throat. "I'm sorry that I didn't take time to get to know you better."

Liam raised an eyebrow giving him a puzzled look.

"So," Padriag continued. "I mean, yeah I know a lot about you. We lived together for centuries. But I don't think you and I ever hung out and talked. You know about deep things."

The curl of his upper lip joined the Brit's raised eyebrow. "Deep things?" Liam's voice laced with impatience. "Seriously, Padriag, what the fuck are you talking about? We've spent many times talking. What can be deeper than the time we were tied together and dragged through the woods naked."

"Ugh," Padriag exclaimed. "I forgot about that. I had to dig rocks out of my ass cheeks after that."

"Or the time," Liam continued, "when those mad villagers caged us and hung us in a tree to die. I believe we spent four or five days getting to know each other pretty well."

"Your hair was never messed up," Padriag replied, "How the hell do you get dragged through the forest by a galloping centaur and not mess up your damn hair?"

His comment ignored, Liam continued, this time smiling at the memory. "Remember the time Gavin and I fought until we practically passed out, and Tristan became so angry he grabbed you and used you like a stick to beat us with?" The Brit let out a laugh. "You screamed like a girl."

"I did not," Padriag retorted, "but that shit did hurt, and it wasn't funny. I don't know why he did that."

Liam shrugged, "he's very strong and you were the closest thing he could reach." The Brit stopped talking and pulled his horse to a stop. A glazed expression came over him and his body went slack, the telltale sign that he had a vision.

They'd not caught up to the guard yet. Alert, Padriag scanned the surroundings. All seemed clear. Other than the sound of the wind through the frozen branches, it was eerily quiet.

"Hurry, we must go." Liam urged his horse to a run and Padriag followed suit. Hopefully the guard had not been attacked.

Padriag would have to wait to ask Liam what he'd seen because right now he was having a hard time keeping up with him.

Whiteness surrounded them. A mixture of snow and ice suddenly blew, making visibility impossible. The horses could not be urged to continue forward. Without vision, the beasts became cautious and frightened. The hair on his nape rose. Padriag began to cast a spell of protection over his small party. Liam turned to give him a thankful half-smile that did not reach his eyes.

"What did you see?" Padriag asked, pulling his sword from the scabbard. "Because I feel something tingling the edge of my ward."

"How strong is your ward?" Liam asked in place of an answer.

"It depends." Padriag replied, catching movement out of the corner of his eye. It looked like one of Meliot's sentinels.

A black wolf. Where there was one, usually more followed. The pack animals never traveled alone.

Liam's horse whinnied and reared when two wolves appeared, blocking the path. The huge beasts did not snarl, but merely seemed to study them, their intelligent eyes scanning their bags.

"Wouldn't happen to have any jerky would you?" Padriag asked Liam. "Maybe they're just hungry."

"I doubt it," Liam replied pulling his sword free. "They are scouts, someone follows." The Brit charged forward towards the wolves, who simple moved out of his way allowing him to pass.

Now that was strange.

Padriag followed suit, but with the lost visibility, they continued their slow trek. The wolves followed at a safe distance.

"We should have caught up with the guard by now," Padriag said glancing back at the wolves.

"Not if they missed this storm, or whatever it is," Liam replied looking about warily. "Look."

They entered a clearing and the snow stopped. It was as if it had never fallen to begin with. They could see clearly again.

It would have been a very good thing if it weren't for being surrounded by black wolves and the woman standing in the middle of the landing waiting for them to dismount.

Which they did, not by choice of course. But with the assistance of her magic, which proved to be very much stronger than Padriag's. He fell to the ground as the woman neared.

Great, it was Meliot's sister, or was it his niece. What was her name? Irene? No, that wasn't it. Elaine? No.

"Ouch!" he screamed when she flung a fireball at him that smarted pretty bad.

"My name is Devina," the beautiful woman told him, her face scrunched in anger. "How dare you forget?"

Padriag stood, back-to-back with Liam, each holding their swords prepared to fight. "Sorry, I have a hard time remembering names sometimes."

She didn't see the humor in his comment. "You won't forget my name again."

Chapter Seventeen

A shift of sorts caused Niall to lose his balance. He managed to stumble a couple of steps without falling. The spell. It must have been the right one. Now he couldn't leave. Not only that, but he didn't know what would happen next.

Could it be true? Was he free from the alter-world. No. It had been too easy.

Not only that, but his wounds revealed that Devina's effects would linger and follow him. Niall slumped against the wall, he held up his hands and studied them as if seeing them for the first time.

He didn't feel any different, neither tired nor rested, but what he could only describe as normal. There did seem to be a grounding of sorts. Other times when he'd come to this world, it was as if he'd not felt connected.

The sensation was totally different this time, which signaled that perhaps he was stuck here in this world. How was it possible? His curse required things that had not happened. He didn't have a family there. His blood went cold. Was it possible Tamara was with child?

The emotions that battled were hard to grasp. Instead of feeling relief, dread lingered. How was it possible that after so many years he was to return to life in Scotland? There had been so many changes. To him it would be as unbelievable as when he'd first been trapped in the alter world. Everything had changed.

Fear overtook to the point that he almost collapsed to his knees. He would have no choice. If this was to be his new world, then he would have to adapt. Easier said than done.

Pushing the tall glass panes open, Niall went out to the balcony, closed his eyes and inhaled. His heart thundered against his breast as questions and emotions continued to swirl in his mind.

Scotland had always been home. The smell of it had not changed over the years. Earthy, lush, and green, the view from the balcony filled him with a mixture of peace and sorrow.

What was he to do now? Scanning the surrounding lands, he saw the cottage that they'd prepared for him. Was that to be his life now?

If Tamara was not with child, he would have to send her away. Tell her to return to her land, back to where she'd lived. The truth of how deeply he felt for her meant he would miss her terribly. The fact that he'd fallen in love with her made him even more resolved to push her away.

Theirs was a doomed relationship. He would not subject her to a marriage with a man that could not sleep for fear of being tortured and one day taken by another woman, whether demon or not. How could he face Tamara after lying with Devina?

At the sound of throat clearing, he turned to see that Tamara had returned. She gave him a quizzical look as if she'd expected that he'd be gone.

Then he felt it, the pull to the other realm. His spirits sank, he wasn't truly free now, but something had definitely changed.

HE WAS STILL THERE but seemed just as resolute to keep her at arm's length. Tammie had enough of trying to guess what the man thought; she was at her wits end with the onslaught of emotions that came whenever she and Niall were together. No matter the depth of physical intimacy they shared, she didn't know him any better than the day they'd met. Could not read his expressions or sense his emotions. His walls were up again, completely repaired from where she managed to chip away at them, even a little.

She studied his wide back as he leaned over the railing outside the French doors. He looked away from her toward the horizon.

He might as well be a million miles away, the distance between them so vast.

Tammie could only watch him while he struggled with his inner demons. Finally, she stepped out of the bedroom and stood next to him.

Without expression or emotion, his gaze flicked over her. He looked away ignoring her.

"I wish you would share your thoughts with me,"

Tammie told him, studying his handsome profile. "You are always so careful to ensure a distance between yourself and others. Is there something I can do? Something I can say to get you to understand that I want to help you. I will listen to whatever it is, no matter how terrible, without judging or even trying to give advice. Sometimes all someone needs is to have a person listen."

She placed her hand on his forearm. He flinched but didn't move away. Nonetheless, his slight movement may as well have been a slap across her face.

Tamara removed her hand from his arm and dropped it to her side. Not sure what to do, part of her wanted to run, to leave, return to Georgia. But the other part, the glutton for punishment part, wanted to keep trying.

She was the only one who could free him. But why should she continue to help this man who refused to help himself?

Should she just give up?

He turned to face her, his eyes vacant. "I don't know how to make you understand, Tamara, I can't ever have a normal life. I won't ever be free. To me, remaining in the enchantment means that I will eventually gain my freedom. Eventually when our time is up, I will die. It is only in death that I will ever truly be a free man."

"I don't understand. What is keeping you from being free and coming here?" Tammie asked him, desperation caused her voice to pitch. "You don't have to stay with me. I don't want you to feel obligated to remain with me."

At his lack of response, she lost her temper. "Maybe you're just not capable of loving."

Niall's darkened eyes locked with hers, his nostrils flared. His body shook as if he struggled to remain calm. "Are you with child?"

She shook her head. "No it is not possible."

His visible relief made her cringe, but then his next words tore into her like a knife.

"Finally you state the truth. I am not capable of love, I am not capable of caring." He clenched his jaw. The muscle on the side of his face pulsed.

Tammie took a step back and held her hands up. "Don't say something you'll regret Niall, I'm warning you."

His gaze did not waiver from hers. The caring she'd seen just minutes earlier when they'd kissed and held each other was completely gone. The man who stood before her was a complete stranger.

He didn't care for her. The acknowledgement was like a punch to her stomach.

If he noticed her distress, he didn't demonstrate it, his stance firm, hands clenched at his sides.

"I can assure you of one thing Tamara; I do not care for you or ever will be capable of loving you."

The slice of pain seared like a hot poker as it cut through her. She stumbled back a couple of steps before gaining enough balance to go to the door. Blindly, she ran down the stairs and made it out past the living room and straight outside. Gulping for air, she stood in the garden, holding on to the short wall, waiting for the dizziness to subside.

"That bastard," she ground out. "I can't believe I love him." Hot tears spilled down her cheeks. This was it, the end of everything. She was done, and more than anything, needed to get away from him. Away from Scotland.

Perhaps it was what her mother had tried to save her from, the worst heartbreak of her life.

While she paced, a light drizzle began to fall. She was glad for it, preferring it to a brighter sunny day. After a few moments, she made two decisions. She'd never speak to or see Niall MacTavish again, and she'd go home.

She entered the house and went directly to the library. Once there, she went to the desk and started the laptop. Tammie prayed as she typed in the familiar website. Let there be a flight that leaves first thing in the morning. Her mother was right. She should have never come to Scotland.

"What's wrong?" Gwen entered the room, a concerned crinkle between her brows. "Have you been crying?"

Tammie nodded. "Yes, I have been bawling my eyes out over that no-good asshole man. And you know what? I'm done, I'm leaving."

Her fingers tapped away as she began to enter the information, her blurry vision making it hard to see the screen.

"Tammie, you can't leave like this. You're too upset. If Niall refuses to be rescued, then he's probably returned to the alter-world by now. He won't return here. Come." Gwen took her hand and pulled her gently to her feet. "Let's talk."

Talk was obviously something she wasn't prepared to do. When she opened her mouth to repeat Niall's cruel words to her sister, she began crying again. Gwen held her, patting her back, telling her all would be all right.

Tammie sat back, accepting a tissue her sister seemed to keep handy. She blew into it, took another one, and wiped at her eyes. "You know the worst part?" A loud sniff interrupted her confession. "I think I'm in love with him. I am in love with a guy that would rather die than be with me!" She fell back against the armrest. "How could I let this happen? I'm an idiot."

"I'm so sorry," Gwen told her, "You're not an idiot. I just can't understand why he said those hurtful things. It's not like him. Niall has always been distant, but from what Tristan says, he rarely said a cross word to them in all those years."

"Well, I guess I brought out the worst in him," Tammie replied, huffing indignantly. "I bring out the jerk in men."

"Oh honey, no you don't." Gwen smiled at her, trying to reassure her.

"I need to return to Atlanta, throw myself into my art, and forget about him." Tammie told Gwen looking back towards the laptop.

"Wait a couple of days at least," Gwen said. "Let's talk it out with Sabrina. At least stay long enough to say goodbye."

"Fine," Tammie grunted, "but don't mention his name, don't talk to me about him and if he reappears, I will not be held responsible if I bash his fool head in."

Her entire body seized, it was as if she'd touched a high voltage wire. Gwen leaned toward her, eyes wide. "What is it?"

"I ... I don't know. But someone needs my help." Tammie closed her eyes to concentrate.

Chapter Eighteen

"Where is he?" Devina approached Padriag, her onyx black eyes boring into him. She kept moving forward ignoring his sword which was pointed directly at her heart. "Where is Niall?"

Padriag wasn't sure how the demon knew Niall's name, but he wasn't about to volunteer information. "Why do you ask about Niall?" he asked instead.

Her dark eyes narrowed and she locked gazes with him for a long moment before her gaze swept over him at a leisurely pace. It made him want to throw up.

"I ask because he belongs to me," she finally replied, continuing to take his measure.

"We don't know where he is," Liam replied, causing her to finally turn her attention away from Padriag.

Devina sneered. "Of course you know where he is. I know the three of you have a bond of sorts. Tell me or die."

Her attention on Liam gave Padriag an opportunity to

mull over what she'd said. That Niall belonged to her. What did that mean?

Devina crossed her arms, her expression softening. It raised the hairs on Padriag's nape. "Either tell me where he is or one of you will take his place and come to me nightly in your sleep."

On the surface, her threat didn't seem that bad, but something about her strange behavior, surrounding them with wolves, not to mention she was Meliot's relative, made him sure these nightly visits wouldn't be pleasurable.

"How long has Niall been going to you?" Liam asked with his usual even tone and bored expression.

Devina pursed her lips. That she answered was surprising. "Almost as long as you've been here in the alter-world."

Good god that explained so much. No wonder Niall was always in a bad mood, sullen and withdrawn. That was why the man rarely slept, and had tried to stay awake most nights until he was too tired to fight it.

"If one of us volunteers, will you free him?" Padriag asked. He may as well do it since he was pretty convinced he was stuck here. Niall didn't deserve this, even if the man didn't leave the alter-world. He'd take his place for the time they had left.

Devina's gaze swept over him again. "I suppose you'd do. You're young and well endowed." Her eyes lingered exactly at the spot she referred to.

Padriag elbowed Liam. "Told you."

"This is not a time to joke," Liam replied. "What the hell are you doing? Don't volunteer for anything."

"Why? Do you want to do it?" Padriag asked.

A growl interrupted their banter, and Padriag realized Devina and the wolves had closed in.

He looked to the beautiful evil being and smiled. "Since we're going to be friends, shouldn't you call off your dogs?"

Straight, even white teeth were revealed when she smiled back. "No, I don't think so. Part of the visits always include a bit of pain. I think I would like to see the both of you mauled. After which I will heal one of you, outwardly only. Perhaps then we will have sex."

"And you expect the man to be aroused. Hmm," Padriag said frowning at Devina. "I can tell you're related to Meliot."

"Attack!" Devina screamed.

NIALL COULD BARELY DEMATERIALIZE. Despite the pull, it was as if he was stuck halfway between the realms.

He wasn't even sure where exactly he should go. He pictured Padriag and Liam and hoped for the best. Finally, the familiar vortex of darkness pulled him in.

The ice crunched under his boots when he appeared. Disoriented, he scanned his surroundings not sure which direction to go. In the sky, two suns were setting, which told him the direction of Atlandia. He began the trek, hoping not to be far from the castle walls so he could avoid Meliot's sentinels or dying of exposure.

Growls echoed, followed by yelling, the voices male. He rushed to a tree and peered around to see what the commotion was about. His eyes widened.

Liam and Padriag fought back-to-back against about a dozen black wolves while Devina watched transfixed. The men seemed to be at a disadvantage. The wolves had some sort of ward of protection around them. Probably Devina's doing.

Both Liam and Padriag were bleeding from bites, but neither seemed to be ready to give up. He drew his sword and rushed out towards them.

At first, his sword seemed to bounce off the first animal he tried to hit, but his second attempt was successful.

"Don't swing the swords," he called to his friends. "Jab at them."

When two wolves fell dead, the rest became wary, circling and waiting for an opening instead, their confidence shaken. The trio of men did the opposite, attacking with more aggression.

A snowstorm began, the sleet falling hard, pelting them vigorously. Devina still watched, leaning forward enjoying the howls of pain from either human or beast. Niall stalked toward her. She was the reason he'd lost Tamara, the reason he'd never be free. The woman would not kill his friends too.

"Call the beasts off," he demanded nearing her, seeing her eyes narrow.

She waved her hands, probably warding against his sword.

"Call them off now Devina."

Her lips curved up, and she looked beyond him to the fight. "He speaks. It's been years since you've spoken to me."

She shrugged her shoulder, a demure movement. "Why should I call them off? I'm enjoying the fight." Her eyes turned back to him, her glare full of venom. "So you have returned. Was she not as exciting as I am?"

He swung his sword aiming for her neck. Although warded, her eyes widened. Her hand flew up, an automatic reflex. The blade bounced back off her protective shield.

Niall lifted his eyebrows, "Not fully confident in your wards, demon?"

With a loud screech, she waved her right hand, and he flew through the air, landing a few feet from where Liam and Padriag held off the remaining wolves. Both seemed to be tiring.

Padriag looked over at him. "She's mad at you."

On his feet again, he stalked back to the woman. "Let them go. It's me you want. I'll stay with you."

Devina cocked her head to the side. "It's too late. The red-haired knight has volunteered to take your place. I think he will be an eager lover." She watched as Padriag leaped back to avoid a dog's bite. "I just might put him in a cage with three wolves tonight before taking him. He has quick reflexes."

"You will do no such thing. He is not taking my place."

"Jealous?" she replied, a bored expression on her face. The fight, it seemed, was not bloody enough for her.

Her eyes snapped back to him. "I am no longer interested in you. You are to die here. Meliot will see to it. I will ask him to gift me Padriag and maybe the blonde one as well."

Rage filled Niall and he yelled, charging towards her, his sword pointing at her heart. Devina held both hands up, no doubt strengthening her ward, but his hit was so direct, she fell backwards.

He jabbed at her, but the protective shield deflected each deathblow, which enraged him further.

Devina jumped up and threw a fireball at him that knocked him against a tree so hard; he knew at least two ribs broke. That did not deter him from rushing her again. This time, when they clashed, she screamed, shocked that he could hit so hard against her ward.

"Watch out behind you!" Padriag yelled.

Niall turned to find two wolves snarling, one was able to bite his calf before he could react. The thud of his sword hitting the beast's side was followed by the animal's death howl. The other wolf flew at his chest knocking him flat on his back. He was able to block a bite to his throat with his arm.

He barely felt the bite or the broken ribs. He'd had plenty of training in degrees of pain, thanks to Devina. The current ones were nothing compared to the years of torture he'd endured in her dungeon. He managed to thrust the beast off of him, hitting the animal's head with the hilt of his sword.

The wolf scrambled to his feet and circled. Devina's amused laughter rang out. Of course she would find his bleeding entertaining. Niall was waiting for the wolf's next attack when he was hit from behind, a direct blow to his nape that knocked him to his knees.

Reeling, he tried to keep focus, barely keeping the sword up. The wolf locked gazes with him, but for some reason did not advance. Devina stepped in front of him. His head swam —he was losing consciousness.

Niall attempted to lift his sword but was too weak from

the last hit. His body refused to obey, a streak of pain radiating through his head.

Padriag and Liam tried to run to him, but snarling wolves blocked them. The men began to fight, but as tired as they were, Niall hoped they could at least defend themselves.

Devina grabbed his sword from his limp hands. "It's a shame really. I had plans for us, for a future together. I have to kill you now. I will be sad, but with your friend's help, I will get over any grief." She actually seemed troubled.

Devina lifted the sword. "I'll make this quick. After all the years of prolonging your agony, why not this farewell gift."

The sword moved toward him and Niall closed his eyes, in spite of everything, he felt ready. His lips curved into a smile, and he waited for death.

The hit didn't register, he fell forward, his body totally limp. A horse whinnied in the distance; instinctively he knew it was his steed, Valor.

Screams sounded, he wasn't sure who it was, and then nothing—complete and total darkness.

Finally, he was free.

THE WOLVES HAD DRIVEN them back until they were unable to go far. The thick bark of trees touched their backs.

Both of Padriag's arms burned from exertion as he continued to jab his sword toward the wolves that seemed to multiply. When one fell, another would materialize and take its place.

Screams sounded, but he couldn't look. Turning away

would give a wolf an opening to attack. Padriag prayed that Niall was continuing to hold his own against Devina. There was little he or Liam could do to help him at the moment.

"Niall, you okay?" Padriag called out. When no answer came, he exchanged looks with Liam, who was bleeding from his right shoulder.

Suddenly, the wolves stopped their attack and backed away. The largest one's silver eyes locked on Padriag with interest.

The wolf gave a short growl, and all of the wolves turned and trotted into the woods, disappearing into the mist.

"What in the bloody hell?" Liam gave him a questioning look.

As one, both swung around to check on Niall.

He lay in the snow, bleeding profusely from a wound to the neck. His horse nudged at him with its nose, and pawed at the ground, his hoof staining the ground red.

Padriag rushed to Niall. Only then did he notice Devina. Or what was left of her a short distance away.

Shocked, he studied the horse. Both of the animal's hooves were bloody, his prints led from where Devina lay to where he stood now. The horse had trampled the demon with its huge hooves. Had not just killed her—but had pummeled her to a mound of bloody flesh.

Liam kneeled on the other side of Niall applying pressure to the wound. "Is he even alive?"

Padriag pressed two fingers on the opposite side of Niall's neck and prayed for a pulse. "He's on the brink of death. His pulse is faint. Looks like Devina meant to behead him. He's lucky her aim was bad, either that or Valor got her just as she made contact."

Neither was sure what to do. Moving Niall could be more detrimental than just covering him and waiting. But it would be almost impossible to survive the Icing.

As if in reply, the wind picked up. The snow laden trees swayed, icicles fell to the ground with heavy thumps.

A sense of foreboding tingled at him and chills traveled over Padriag's arms. "We need to get out of here. Meliot is going to be seriously pissed at Devina's death. We have to carry Niall and get the hell out of here."

"I agree," Liam replied looking around.

They managed to wrap a thick strap of fabric around Niall's neck. Thankfully, the bleeding had slowed. Once satisfied that Niall was at least stable, Padriag rounded up the horses and cast a spell of warmth over all of them as Liam picked up Niall.

"We should go to the other realm. They have better healing there," Padriag stated. The men closed their eyes, both trembling from the cold and exhaustion. Using what was left of their already depleted energy they dematerialized.

THEY APPEARED NEAR THE STABLES. Padriag looked around in confusion. Whoa, we brought the horses, he thought. He eyed the animals, who didn't seem affected in the least. One even lowered its head and sniffed the grass. "Not my first choice," he said. "I think Niall's welfare is more important than housing the horses."

Liam shrugged, "I didn't do it. Probably your spell."

Padriag slipped his hands more securely under Niall's underarms and Liam lifted his feet. Much to their relief, Tristan pulled up in a golf cart, his eyes rounding at seeing them and the horses.

"You brought the horses?" Gavin ran out from the stables. "What happened?"

Both waved off any answers, their concentration on the unconscious Niall.

"A demon named Devina tried to kill Niall," Padriag informed them. "We need to get him to a doctor."

The men loaded Niall onto the motorized cart. Tristan pulled out his cell phone and called ahead as they sped to the main house. Padriag didn't like how pale Niall was becoming. Could it be that, after all this, Niall would not survive?

He leaned over placing his ear to Niall's chest. His heartbeat was weak but steady which relieved him somewhat.

The women came outside as they arrived. Tammie went straight to Niall, her eyes widening at the sight of his injuries. "Oh my god."

Both Sabrina and Gwen studied Padriag and Liam. "What happened to y'all?"

Padriag realized they all probably looked like hell, bleeding from wolf bites, battered and bruised.

The woman from the castle, Erin, stood at the doorway, not coming closer. Her pale blue eyes scanned over him, then to the others.

Gwen peered at Niall, her eyes large with worry. "A doctor is on his way. He said it was quicker for him to come here since he was not that far.

"We should insist on a hospital instead." Tammie replied placing her hand on Niall's brow. "He's awfully pale."

Tristan shook his head. "I think we should take him inside. Let's see what the doctor says. Niall is very strong."

They moved Niall into the house and lay him on a bed in a guestroom on the first floor, barely getting him settled when the doctor rushed in with a nurse in tow and made them leave the room.

Padriag moved into the hallway with the others. He was ushered into the kitchen along with Liam. "We need to check your injuries. Both of you will need cleaning and bandaging."

"I am fine. Just need a good hot shower," Padriag said as the room seem to tilt. Next thing he knew, his face was smushed into the rug. It seemed he'd fallen face-first onto the floor.

"Ow," he mumbled. "That hurt."

<hr>

A SOFT LIGHT ebbed into the edges of a swirling darkness. Niall tried to move, to see more than shades of gray, but it proved impossible. It was as if he floated, his body not truly anchored to a solid place.

Voices permeated the haze, and he tried to turn, to speak, but that too was unsuccessful

"I think we should wait and tell him once he recovers," Liam's voice said.

"That's stupid, he'll figure it out right away," Gavin spoke next in a hoarse whisper.

"Should we tie him up first, in case he decides to get violent?" Padriag, the ass, spoke next.

"He may not take it well, but nothing can be done about it now," Tristan stated, his tone not giving away whatever they spoke about.

Again he fought, trying to climb from whatever pit he seemed to be stuck in.

Hoping to be heard, he tried to talk.

"What are you going to tell me?" Niall croaked and immediately began coughing. It felt as if his throat was filled with sand.

Again he tried to pry his eyes open, he needed to see if it was all a perverse trick of fate. He'd died and in his afterlife had been sent back to the alter-world. In this world, all the men he'd been trapped with for decades existed.

So much for his freedom.

"Say something, somebody," Padriag told the room. "He may as well know."

Someone cleared his throat, and Niall finally could stand it no longer. He fought against what felt like stones on his eyelids and managed to open his eyes. The world was a blurry place, nothing was clear.

Again he tried to talk but his throat seemed to collapse, and another coughing fit began.

A cup of water was placed up to his mouth and he drank from it with greed. More was poured and he emptied that one as well.

The surroundings became clearer, and he could see his four friends watching him with interest.

Liam and Padriag stood at the foot of his bed, while

Tristan and Gavin stood on both sides. None of them spoke; instead they seemed to be waiting for him to say something.

"I need time to …" Niall lay back on the pillow and stared up at the ceiling. To what? Did he want to prolong not knowing? And for how long?

"Where am I and what are you supposed to tell me?" he managed to ask in a husky voice. Lifting up to his elbows, he immediately regretted it when his head swam. Still he refused to lay back down.

Three sets of eyes looked to Tristan who seemed to be voted the spokesperson for the group. The Laird clenched his jaw, but when he looked at Niall, his expression softened.

"Niall, your enchantment has been broken. You are free. You are here in modern-day Scotland with us."

Padriag interrupted, a wide grin splitting his face. "You did it, you're free."

Liam and Gavin both smiled at him, but he saw wariness in Liam's eyes. *Trouble ahead?*

"No." He didn't want to say it, but they had to know the truth. "I cannot be totally free. There is something else holding me to the alter-world …" he began.

"Devina, yes we know," Tristan interrupted him. "She insinuated to Padriag that you had been her victim for many years."

Niall nodded mutely.

"Devina is dead," Liam told him.

"Valor attacked Devina," Padriag said, referring to his horse. "It was as if the horse was more powerful than her magic. No matter what she tried to throw at him, nothing affected him."

"It was like nothing we've ever seen," Liam added. "There was nothing left of her, but a pile of flesh and black blood."

A ringing began in his ears, and trembling took over his body, darkness threatened as the room began to spin, but he held on, took a deep breath and blew the air out.

"I think he's hyperventilating," Padriag told the group.

Someone placed something on his face and told him to take deep breaths. He batted the object away.

"I am fine. What happened to Valor?"

"We brought him with us," Padriag told him.

The men continued to watch him as the information sunk in.

He was free.

A violent storm of emotions swirl in his chest as he fought to breathe normally. The air didn't settle in his lungs as scenarios flew through his mind. Devina was dead. Somehow he was free.

"How?"

"You have been asleep for a week, err, sennight," Tristan told him. "Tamara continually chanted a spell over you."

"Tamara?" He searched the men's faces. "What about the terms of my curse. A sacrifice of fate? What of family? I do not understand."

"We are your family, dumbass," Padriag said, leaning over him and helping him drink more water. "About fate, that part, I believe has to do with Tamara."

He'd said terrible things to Tamara. She would never forgive him. Another thought struck, and he inhaled sharply at the pang in his chest.

"What did she do?' Niall managed to croak out. "Tell me."

"She willingly gave up all her magical powers," Liam said. "She claimed it wasn't a huge sacrifice in comparison to you being free."

"And she's gone back to her home, across the ocean," Gavin added.

Niall closed his eyes, unable to absorb everything.

He was free.

Tamara was gone.

Chapter Nineteen

The roaring sounds of the mechanical contraption he was trapped in hummed and sent vibrations though the entire craft. Niall clenched the arm of the chair he was strapped into, closed his eyes, and held his breath. This was not natural. Man was not intended to fly in something that wasn't even alive.

The airplane, as they'd called it, had no connection to the world, no fear of plummeting. At least when flying on a dragon one knew the beast did not want to splat onto the ground below, not on purpose at least.

"Are you all right?" Sabrina, Tamara's sister, asked him and placed her hand over his. "I imagine it's pretty terrifying to fly in an airplane for the first time." He opened his eyes and glanced at her. She smiled, but the lines of worry remained on her brow. "Once we reach a cruising altitude, er ... height, it will be smoother. The pilot, Derrick, has a lot of experience."

She referred to the man who guided the metal dragon.

Derrick was related to Tristan, and he not only favored the Laird, but had the same stubborn, self-assured personality as his ancestor.

Derrick McRainey arrived just that morning announcing they'd leave within an hour to America. Evidently. Tristan not only had a huge fortune, but he also owned a private airplane, which Derrick flew.

The flight did not seem to affect Liam, who sat across from them sipping a drink and reading a glossy book. The Brit appeared to be relaxed.

The airplane finally stopped climbing and leveled off. Sabrina was right, the movement seemed smoother. They'd be flying for ten hours at least, so he took a deep calming breath. It helped, but not much. He frowned at Liam. "Why are you flying with us? You could have just stayed back."

With a slight shrug, Liam replied. "I might as well get used to the new way of travel. It's cumbersome don't you think? It's going to be an adjustment not to be able to will ourselves elsewhere."

He gave Sabrina a crooked grin. "John is there for a book event and is excited about meeting me at the port."

"Airport," Sabrina corrected him. "Atlanta is a huge city; there is so much to do. You'll love it. I believe it's like London at its height when you lived there."

Niall wondered if he'd like living there. He wasn't sure what Tamara would demand in exchange for forgiving him. He'd prefer to return to Scotland, but at this point he couldn't ask for anything. The most he could hope for was that she agree to be part of his life. If she wished to remain in America, so would he.

"Have you thought about what you're going to say to her?" Sabrina asked, studying him. "When she left, Tammie was set on never seeing you again and not returning to Scotland until able to be around you. You hurt her Niall, and she's a very proud person. I hope you can change her mind."

"I hope so too. What can I do but hope that she cares enough for me to hear my explanation." He gratefully accepted a glass of wine from a male attendant.

"I think, she will not only forgive you, but I believe she'll agree to return to Scotland as well." Liam remarked, stretching. How the man could be so relaxed was baffling.

"Is this a vision?" Niall asked.

Liam shook his head. "I don't seem to have them when I'm in this realm."

If his fate was to live alone in Scotland with his friends and his horse, then it was more than he could have ever hoped for. Still, he wanted Tamara to be part of it.

THE ODD THING about wet paint was that when she flung a still fresh canvas across the room, it made an interesting pattern. Once again she flicked the brush, speckles flying onto the canvas.

Tammie blew her bangs off her forehead and put her brushes down. In one week, she was to take part in an art expo. So far she only had four paintings.

She'd agreed to have at least eight. The green landscape she'd been working on was an abstract of a Scottish landscape. Shades of green under a grayish blue sky with bright slashes of brownish shades cutting between.

She bent and picked it up, putting it back on the easel. She cocked her head to the side. It didn't help. What had been a mediocre effort at best was now ugly. She shouldn't have flung the orange paint on it. Sweeping her arm across, her wrist collided with the edge of the canvas sending it onto the floor.

Tammie stormed from the room and passed through the darkened townhouse without noticing how empty and quiet it was.

Sabrina always kept the house fully lit, loving the ambiance of the different lamps and other light fixtures she and Gwen had collected over the years. There were spotlights for Tammie's artwork, blown glass lamps that hung over the kitchen counters; Tiffany style lighting usually warmed the sitting area in the living room.

In her bedroom, she made a beeline for the bathroom, not wanting to get any paint on her bedding or rugs.

Once in the shower, she allowed the hot water to wash over her, relieving the stress of her muscles. She turned her back to the steamy flow and hung her head so that her spine stretched under the massaging water. She'd finally spoken with her mother and explained about her powers and losing them.

There was a different feel to her body, it was as if she had to learn to use her arms and legs again. It was lighter in a way, as if she'd lost pounds off her limbs. The magic was gone, the moment is had happened, when she'd transferred it to Valor, she'd felt it drain from every pore, every inch. Strange sensations akin to strings being pulled from under her skin had left her raw, barely able to stand touch.

When she'd faced her sisters, they'd immediately known.

"This is what mother was afraid of," Gwen said. "That you'd give up everything if you came to Scotland."

Sabrina had given her a knowing look. "The sacrifice."

Needing to reassure her mother, Tammie had called and told her everything. Between sniffs, her mother told her how relieved she was that the sacrificed she'd foreseen was not what she'd feared. Apparently, she'd had recurring dreams of Tammie being trapped in another realm never to return.

Then her mother had asked about Niall and what would happen next. Tammie had been vague in her answer. "Time will tell."

Niall had been asleep when she'd walked into the room to see him for the last time.

At that point, she'd figured out how to break the curse. Calling the men into the room, she'd chanted the spell and had them repeated it. Then holding her hands up, she'd surrendered her magic to the universe.

A strong whirlwind had swept the room, then it was silent. When she tried to form a fireball, nothing happened.

"He's free," Liam had announced, and the others nodded. Apparently, a surge of energy swept through them each time one of them was freed.

Just thinking about the last weeks in Scotland made her tired. No, she was not ready to think about Scotland, which in turn meant her thoughts would immediately turn to him.

She climbed into bed and closed her eyes, the soft sound of traffic outside lulling her to sleep.

"Tammie," A voice hissed, "are you asleep?"

"What?" Tammie bolted up banging foreheads with Sabrina. "Ow!" They both yelped.

"You scared the shit out of me. What are you doing here?" Tammie squinted at the now-lit room. "And why in the hell did you turn on the bright overhead light?"

Sabrina smiled; she looked refreshed, at midnight. Only her sister would look that good in the middle of the night. "I came to see you. We're worried about you. You left so quickly."

Her expression changed, eyes sliding to the doorway, lips curving into a mischievous smile. "I brought you a present too."

Tammie narrowed her eyes, peering at Sabrina's hands. "I don't see any present."

"Oh, no silly, you have to get dressed and come out to the living room. It's too big to carry." Sabrina giggled, her eyes twinkling, which made Tammie more suspicious.

"Why do I have to be dressed?" It didn't make sense unless there were people in the living room. It's not some sort of surprise party is it?"

Sabrina gave her an innocent wide-eyed look. "I'm not saying anything else." She turned on her heel and practically ran out of the room.

Only Sabrina would think a surprise party in the middle of the night was something she'd enjoy. As much as she detested the idea of a party, she was too nosy to remain in bed.

She would not get dressed. The people would be

subjected to her bright pink tank top and bikini panty set. She'd say hello and go back to bed.

"That will teach them," she mumbled, padding toward the living room in bare feet.

The living room was gloomy and empty. Only one lamp was lit. She stood for a moment tapping her bare foot.

"Sabrina?"

No one replied.

"This isn't funny. If people are going to jump out and say surprise, do it now or I'm going back to bed."

Still no one answered.

She turned and inspected the empty kitchen. Where the hell did Sabrina go? "I'm going back to bed sister. Your joke is lame." She turned to go back to the bedroom. The sound of the back door shutting caused her to turn.

Niall stood by the back door. Although she could not see his face clearly, she recognized him. His stance was rigid, which made her wonder if Sabrina had forced him to come. This was not her idea of a good present. Once again, Niall forced to do something against his will.

He didn't want to leave the enchantment, his love so great for his wife that he'd rather remain in the alter-world and die to be with her. He sure as hell did not want to be with Tammie. But, knowing her conniving sisters, they'd played on his honor code and told him being with her was the right thing to do. Now here he stood, looking like he'd rather be anywhere but.

"Hello, Tamara." He always called her Tamara, pronouncing it like no one else, but somehow it sounded like a caress when he said it. The sound of his voice wrapped over her like a warm blanket. "How are you?" He came closer, and she could see the discomfort in his expression. She felt sorry for him.

"Niall, you didn't have to fly here. I know that was probably not a pleasant experience," Tammie told him. He didn't respond, only watched her, his grey eyes scanning over her, hesitating at seeing the panties.

She felt naked in her skimpy pajamas and went to the kitchen needing to place the counter between them. For once she should have listened to Sabrina and gotten dressed.

"Look, I know my sisters can be convincing. They manipulated you into coming here and marrying me by taking advantage of the knight's honor code, didn't they?"

"No," he replied watching her with intensity. "I did not have to be forced to come here."

Of course he would not admit to being forced. "So why are you here then? Did you suddenly decide that you are capable of caring for me? Because last time we talked you were pretty fervent about how you could never feel anything for me."

"Forgive me." The sincerity in his eyes made her believe he was sorry for hurting her feelings.

She shrugged, pretending it was nothing. "You can't help how you feel. You don't have to apologize. Granted, you didn't have to be so harsh, but then again, you left no room for any misunderstanding."

"I need you to listen to me." He came around the counter and reached for her but lowered his arm at her lifting her hands up to stop him. "Will you allow me to explain?"

As it was, she fought to keep her emotions in check. She

wanted to touch him. Her mind and body craved his touch. She wanted to cry, allow the tears to finally fall, tell him how much she missed him. How she'd agree to anything as long as he stayed with her. But it would not work. He didn't love her, and she would not force him to remain with her out of a sense of honor.

"I can't, Niall. There is nothing you can say that will convince me your feelings have changed so drastically in such a short period."

"My feelings for you have never changed."

"At least you're honest." She turned away from him to hide the tears that threatened. Damn him and her nosy sisters. "Please go."

He didn't move so she went around him. "Fine. Stay if you want. Do whatever you want. I'm going back to bed. Tell Sabrina her present sucked."

Tammie ran to her bedroom and crawled into the bed, tears falling. Sorrow cut painfully through the layers of protection she'd tried to build. If only she didn't love him so completely, it wouldn't hurt as much.

The bed dipped and strong arms surrounded her, pulling Tammie against him. She wanted to argue and push him away, but it was no use. She could never resist his touch.

He kissed her hair and softly urged her to calm. "Tamara don't cry. I am so very sorry for hurting you," Niall pleaded. "I needed to protect you. That is why I said those things."

As much as she knew it was best to move away, Tammie didn't stir, it felt so good to just allow him to hold her.

"There was more to my imprisonment than the enchantment you see," Niall continued, "I was also trapped by

Devina, a trap that even here I could not escape. I could not sentence you to a marriage with someone who could not sleep for fear of being taken to her dungeon and her bed."

He kissed her again and, placing his hand under her chin, turned her face up to him. "Believe me when I tell you that hurting you was as painful for me as it was for you. But I saw no other way."

Tammie waited until she could finally speak without blubbering. She took a deep cleansing breath. "Why are you telling me all of this now? Has something changed with that bitch?"

"She's dead," Niall told her, his voice filled with hatred. "A death that did not do justice to what she truly deserved."

"Are you sure she's dead?"

"I have not been pulled into her realm. I have waited to be sure I would not be drawn away by her before coming here. I believe she is truly dead."

"Oh," was the only response Tammie could manage before continuing. "Those were your two cages then."

"Aye, I'm free. Two cages were Meliot and Devina. Her death along with McMurray's spell and your sacrifice..." He hesitated, his eyes misting, "it broke the enchantment."

"What if one of the cages was the love that tethers you to your wife? You wanted to reunite with her. Wasn't that one of the reasons you resisted being rescued?"

His eyes went soft, and lips curved into a barely there smile. "I will never stop loving Caitlin or thinking of my children. However, they are my past, another lifetime. You, Tamara, are my present."

Tammie was not sure what to think. "What do you wish for now?" Her breath caught, waiting for his answer.

"I want you in whatever way you allow," he replied. "In exchange, I offer you all of me. I love you Tamara Lockhart."

For the first time in her life, Tammie was struck silent.

"Do you have nothing to say?" Niall asked.

She shook her head, took his face in her hands, and pulled his lips to hers.

His response was ardent, his lips covering hers. She felt him relax and fall with her onto the bed. When his tongue began to explore her mouth, she ran her hands through his hair. Niall's hands moved down her side and he caressed her back and butt, each touch filling her with heat and want.

Her limited clothing was gone before she knew it. He removed his with haste and when he held her to him, she reveled in the feel of his hard body pressed to hers. They lay side by side, his hardness teasing her as he tasted her skin, kissing her neck, shoulders, and breasts.

They made love with urgency, with passion, with greed.

Everything disappeared except each other, the sounds of their lovemaking, harsh breaths, and sounds of suckling both lips and skin.

Their movements became almost frantic racing toward the crest from which the fall would be ever so magical.

In that moment, Tammie understood what it meant to be fully loved. Niall loved every part of her, body, mind, and soul.

To her, he was perfection, their bodies recognizing the other half, the only partner each would ever require. Nothing else could possibly reach the level of sensations, the heights that they reached together.

Just as she began to climb, Tammie met Niall's gaze. "I love you."

In response, he inhaled deeply, his eyes falling closed. "And I love you."

His movements continued, and with each plunge, he urged her closer to release until stars exploded behind her eyelids. The sound of his release, the hoarse deep moan as his entire body shuddered, sent her to float with him.

They lay silent, both caressing the other, not wanting to break the spell of their reunion.

He sighed contentedly and kissed her neck. This tall, handsome, mostly silent man who she loved belonged to her now.

Tammie couldn't stop smiling.

He rolled off of her, but held her tightly against his

"Do you love me?" Niall asked.

She caressed his face. "I love you with all my being."

"Will you marry me?"

The question caught her off guard. "Uh ... Are you sure?" she stuttered.

"Of course I am sure."

"Well I am certainly not going to allow you to run around this realm single and looking so medieval and hot. Women are going to throw themselves at you."

"I do not know what you said." He kissed her lightly. "Is that a yes?"

"Yes," Tammie replied trailing her hand down his chest past his stomach. "Oh yes."

Epilogue

"Shh, love," Tammie cooed at the baby, soothing the infant while digging in her bag for a bottle. The child eagerly took to it when she popped it into his mouth.

She watched from a short distance away as Niall stood looking over the large expanse of the headstones at the cemetery in a village called Dunbeg, which had been called Dunstaffnage when Niall lived there. Many of the headstones were so old the engraving was illegible, yet somewhere here his first wife and children were buried.

Peace radiated in this place, the area surrounded by trees of many types, each casting a different hue of green forming a beautiful background. Tammie swayed the now sleepy baby and kept a concerned eye on Niall. He hadn't moved in a while, seemed to be praying so she didn't call out to him.

Since returning to Scotland, they'd lived in the cottage on the castle lands while building a house on lands Tristan had sold to them.

The large home was to have four bedrooms, two sitting rooms, a large kitchen and dining room. Also, there would be a studio for her on the side of a hill where she could study the lush green vegetation while she painted.

They'd conceived Baby Neal in Atlanta. Tammie was sure of it, because exactly nine months almost to the day, she'd gone into labor.

Baby Neal's arrival came with a torrent of activity, both her sisters and their partners insisting on going to the hospital with them. There was no argument that changed their minds since Tammie had the bad luck to go into labor while they celebrated Sabrina and Gavin's small wedding.

So, along with her and Niall, John, Liam and Gwen and Tristan, the new bride and groom all caravanned to the hospital where the nurses were beside themselves, not only because of the size of the group but because the five most handsome men in the village happened to be in the same room at the same time.

One nurse was so overcome she'd fainted upon handing a cup of water to Gavin. The poor man caught her and spilled said water over both of them, which brought hysterical laugher from the others. An older nurse finally placed a surgical mask over Gavin's face so that the younger nurses could concentrate on their patients.

It did little good. It seemed every woman in the village was suddenly sick, or visiting a patient that day.

Niall stayed alongside her the entire time. He paled when the baby appeared but made her proud by not passing out.

Unfortunately, Gavin, who insisted on also being in the room, did.

The memories made it impossible not to smile. Each time Tammie remembered the trip to the hospital and all the chaos, she grinned.

After placing the sleeping baby in the tram, Tammie pressed a kiss to his downy cheek. The baby's black hair fluttered in the warm breeze. Love filled her and she could not tear her eyes from him.

When she turned to see about Niall, he remained where he was. But was now looking over at her. A smile spread across his face, and he walked toward her.

Tammie looked past him toward the gravestones. "You found them. I am glad."

"As am I."

Her eyes filled with tears at his happy smile.

"Beatrice lived to be sixty, a long life for that time. Which means, she must have had a happy life, to live so long."

"Of course she did," Tammie agreed.

Niall nodded. "I feel at peace. At least for myself. I still worry about Padriag. Meliot will eventually attack or harm him. I am sure."

"We will find a way to free him. I think I know who will free him. We just have to convince her."

"Erin," they both said at the same time and sighed. Erin was having a hard time. She'd convinced herself going to the alter-world had been some sort of illusion, and therefore what had happened was not real. Not only did they have to bring her around to believing it really happened, but somehow persuade her to save Padriag.

"She will come around," Tammie assured Niall, while praying it was true.

For a long moment, they stood looking over the land. It was serene.

"We best go," Tammie said.

"Aye, I have to speak to the builder before he leaves for the day," Niall said and peered down at their slumbering child. "I think to want more bairns."

"Oh really," Tammie laughed. "Well, you're lucky you married a young lass like me, you old man."

His chuckle was deep. When he laughed, it still caught her by surprise. Finally, Niall was truly a free man.

THE THREE MOONS remained in the sky. For some reason, they lingered longer than anyone had predicted. However, Padriag didn't pay them any mind. For almost a year he'd remained in the alter-world alone.

Liam did return to stay for a few days here and there, for which Padriag was thankful, but it wasn't the same.

Since being the last one trapped, time had seemed to slow to a snail's pace, each day lingering, the nights not coming soon enough.

Padriag had taken to painting, a hobby he'd not tried before. He considered photography, but after managing to bring cameras from the other realm, he found that they didn't work there.

After a few months in Atlandia, he'd returned to the keep. For some reason, Meliot and his minions hadn't bothered him since, but Padriag wasn't fooled. Sooner or later the wizard would strike, and he had to be prepared.

Making his way down the stairs after sleeping in as long as possible, he was greeted by the view of Liam setting the table.

"I made a full English," the Brit said. "The best meal ever invented."

Padriag rolled his eyes, "I prefer a full Scottish."

"What's the difference?" Liam asked. "Lack of taste in the Scottish one?"

In truth the food smelled delicious, but he couldn't keep from teasing Liam. "It's missing tattie scones."

While they ate, Liam informed him about the progress they'd been making in assuring his freedom. Padriag barely listened. For the past months nothing had worked. In fact, it seemed to be doing more harm than good. He was finding it harder and harder to travel between the realms.

"You must come to the other realm in a sennight. There is a plan in place that Gwen, John and Sabrina are working on. They are sure it could work."

"Could," Padriag said, his eyes flashing to the windows as a shadow crossed outside. "I will do my best to be there. Right now we must prepare. It seems either Meliot has sent something to spy on us, or perhaps I've acquired a pet dragon."

Both men hurried to the window and peered out.

A familiar creature circled the keep, its huge wings moving with grace.

"That's Sterling's beast," Liam murmured.

A parchment floated in the air landing just outside the door, then the magnificent beast flew away.

Padriag hurried to the door and opened it. After insuring

there was no one about, he fetched the rolled parchment and went back inside.

He read over it and then read it again.

"What does it mean?" Liam asked scanning the words probably for a third time.

"An invitation to live in his realm until I am freed," Padriag replied. "It means Meliot has recovered from whatever the dragon did to him and will come after me with guns blazing."

Liam let out a long breath. "We best get packing then. Looks like we're moving to Esland."

"We?" Padriag scowled at the Brit.

"I've always wanted to see it." Liam raced up the stairs probably to pack.

Padriag trudged up the stairs. "We don't have horses, remember, they're in the other realm."

Liam turned to look at him. "Your adventure begins my friend."

Struan

The Sea Lion

The Sea Lord

Laurel Creek Series

Jaded: Luke

Brash: Frederick

Broken: Taylor

Ruined: Tobias

Brides for All Seasons

Christina

Sarah

Wilhelmina

Aurora

Lucille

Esther

Scarlet

Isabel

Montana Cowboys

Montana Bachelor

Montana Boss

Montana Beau

Montana Bred

Montana Born

Montana Born & Bred

The Lass and the Laird

Lady and the Scot

The Laird's Daughter

Highland Medieval Romance

Highlander - The Archer

The Duke's Fiery Bride

Contemporary & Western Romance

Melody of Secrets

Taming Lisa

Cowboy in Paradise

About the Author

USA Today* bestselling author *Hildie McQueen brings action, romance, and unique settings to life in her captivating stories. From sweeping Scottish historical romance to thrilling contemporary romances, her books offer something for every reader to devour!

When she's not weaving tales, Hildie loves diving into a good book, connecting with fans at events, exploring new places, and spending time with her three adorable pups. She lives in the charming small town in Georgia with her superhero husband, Kurt, who makes every day an adventure.